I0620841

FEET
TO
THE
STARS

ABOUT THE AUTHOR

Susan Midalia is the author of two collections of short stories: *A History of the Beanbag*, shortlisted for the Western Australian Premier's Book Awards, and *An Unknown Sky*, shortlisted for the Steele Rudd Award. She is also a freelance editor and a facilitator of workshops in short story writing. She has a PhD in contemporary Australian women's fiction and has published on the subject in national and international literary journals.

Praise for *An Unknown Sky and other stories*

… beautifully written and never over-written… Midalia is a master of inference drawn from detail.
Australian Book Review

Midalia's skill at presenting big ideas through everyday experience demonstrates how powerful good writing can be.
West Australian

… stories that unerringly and gracefully obtain rare vantage points on life.
The Australian

Praise for *A History of the Beanbag and other stories*

Susan Midalia is particularly good with life's awkwardnesses, especially as endured by the innocent or naïve…Deep in the heart of the most comfortable suburbia there's a faulty valve, and Midalia is adept at finding it."
The Australian Literary Review

… remarkably accomplished at showing how it feels to grapple with the incubi of ordinariness behind drawn Venetian blinds…this writer abolishes ordinariness by showing that it is usually extraordinary if you consider it attentively…her gifts are those of a remarkable poise and clarity of manner, and an economy and range in storytelling which sustains interest from first to last…Susan Midalia deserves to be read by the widest possible audience.
Adelaide Review

These are finely crafted and carefully observed stories about ordinary life in suburban settings.
Sydney Morning Herald

FEET
TO
THE
STARS

AND
OTHER
STORIES

SUSAN
MIDALIA

UWA PUBLISHING

First published in 2015 by
UWA Publishing
Crawley, Western Australia 6009
www.uwap.uwa.edu.au

UWAP is an imprint of UWA Publishing,
a division of The University of Western Australia.

THE UNIVERSITY OF
WESTERN AUSTRALIA
Achieve International Excellence

The following stories were originally published elsewhere:

'The Hook' in *Southerly*, Vol. 74:1, 2014

'A Blast of a Poem' in *Australian Love Stories 2104*, C. Kennedy (ed.),
Inkerman & Blunt, 2014

'The Inner Life' in *Westerly*, Vol. 59:2, November 2014

This book is copyright. Apart from any fair dealing for the purpose of private
study, research, criticism or review, as permitted under the *Copyright Act 1968*,
no part may be reproduced by any process without written permission.
Enquiries should be made to the publisher.

Copyright © 2015 by Susan Midalia

The moral right of the author has been asserted.

We gratefully acknowledge permission to quote an extract from the poem "You're", by
Sylvia Plath, © 1965, from the volume *Ariel*, first published by Faber and Faber in 1965.

National Library of Australia Cataloguing-in-Publication data:
Midalia, Susan.
Midalia, Susan, author.
Feet to the stars and other stories / Susan Midalia.
ISBN: 9781742587547 (paperback)
Short stories.
A823.4

Typeset in 11 pt Bembo by Lasertype
Printed by Griffin Press

This project has been assisted by the Australian Government
through the Australia Council, its arts funding and advisory body

To my mother
Michaela

Contents

The Hook

Despite her fleecy jacket and fur-lined gloves, a long woollen scarf wound tightly round her neck, she could feel the cold seeping into her bones. And after trudging six long blocks into a headwind, those bones, and her teeth, were beginning to ache. But here she was, at last, standing right in front of it: the building she'd admired in photos and postcards, this art deco wonder in praise of the car. Automobile, they called it here.

Marina craned her neck to take it all in: the needle-thin spire piercing the sky and, just below, the terraced crown, like gorgeous rays of the sun. She saw gleaming steel walls adorned – ingeniously, audaciously – with replicas of radiator caps. And those famous gargoyles, the sleek heads of eagles, staring boldly, implacably, across the city. She'd read about the maniacal race to be the tallest building in New York; and for just a few months, before the rise of the Empire State and other hurried monuments to power, this beautiful Chrysler Building had been proudly undefeated – the Mount Everest of Manhattan, they'd called it. She couldn't remember its height, even though she'd read it in the guidebook. Connor would have remembered, would have known the exact number of eagles and radiator caps as well; even, perhaps, the number of bricks and rivets that went into its magical making. He'd always been drawn to quantify and measure: height and width, length and depth, dates and statistics, the number of items in museums. Awed by the sublime; amused by the folly of excess.

She stood back and took several photos with her phone. Checked them and zoomed in closer, took several more. She'd promised her sister that she'd keep a record, have some people round for a slide show. A few drinks.

Connor would have loved this building, she thought. Its shimmering elegance, its emblematic faith in the future. He would gladly have walked as she had walked, on crowded pavements, into galleries and museums, through Central Park, with its ghostly trees set against a wintry sky. He'd always been an energetic traveller, walking for miles around the deep red walls of Marrakesch; scaling hills and striding meadows in the Lake District; happily wandering for hours in the maddening maze of Venice, when she thought she would faint in the sapping heat and the rotting smells from the canals, the press of so many tourists, but she'd done it in the end without complaining. Back in the hotel he'd put his arms around her and called her a trooper, *my trooper, my darling*, and kissed her, laid her down on the bed and made love to her. And she missed this, too. Unbearably. His sculptured hipbones; the sprinkle of freckles across his shoulders; his playful, tender, searching hands; the greying hair on his chest. In the beginning, when they made love and he was spent with sex, she would lie in their bed and marvel at the weight of his arm sprawled carelessly on a pillow; at the tiny flickers of his eyelashes, butterfly dreams on his cheeks. The way the early morning sun drifting through the curtain made moving shadows on his flesh. She would watch all this with the eyes of a languorous woman, tracing a finger over his back or thighs, lightly, so as not to wake him. She had never spoken of this to anyone. Because it was far too intimate and precious, and because no one had ever asked her. Maybe one day someone would ask her. *What do you remember, Marina?* her sister might say, leaning across a table, stroking her hand.

She remembered hanging out the washing in the dead of night and looking up at a moonless sky. She remembered crying out to no one and to nothing: *You're gone.*

Her family had been pleased about her trip, but anxious that she was travelling alone. Marina had lied that none of her friends could take any time off work; and she'd lied by omission as well, couldn't tell them of Connor's longing to see the city that never sleeps. How he'd started reading books, piles of them from the library, and checking tourist sites online. *All the museums*, he'd declared. *It'll take a lifetime.* And top of the list, he'd said in his charming Irish lilt, was a place called Ellis Island. The most famous immigration centre in the world, he'd said, and given her a raft of numbers: the date of its founding, the millions of people who'd arrived there from so many countries, the numbers of rooms and exhibits. But two years on, standing in front of this building, people rushing past, bumping into her, *excuse me, Ma'am*, feeling slightly dizzy now, all she could remember was the brightness of his eyes as he looked up from a book;

his unstoppable, puppy-dog bouncing at life. Her guide, her lover, her heart's delight. So she didn't, couldn't, tell her parents, her sister, anyone at all, of her need to travel alone. To pay tribute to his memory. To compensate, perhaps. Or atone. It was something private, she knew, like the meeting of two bodies in a bed. Nor could she tell them how she longed for silence. For it sometimes seemed to her, more and more it seemed to her, that people proclaimed their opinions, dispensed advice, gossiped, condemned, maligned, consoled, talked and talked their full-of-nothing words like so much litter blowing in the wind.

The cold was beginning to bite again and she needed to gather herself up, move on to Carnegie Hall. Someone at work had a cousin with a son whose friend had once played there, and this seemed as good a reason as any to visit. Take a few photos. And as she struggled forward, she felt that, after all, she didn't really mind the cold, that she almost welcomed it: this rude buffeting, this icy assailment. For it gave her back the edges, the sharp definition, that she sometimes felt dissolving in the blackness of the night.

She looked around her hotel room: neat and clean, with the basics — a bed, a desk and chair, a bar fridge, a kettle and a tiny TV. A frayed brown carpet. Three stars; entirely adequate. The kind of place they'd always chosen on their travels.

She flopped down on the bed, exhausted with walking and all the blathering at Carnegie Hall, vexed by the tour she'd had little choice but to join. *Oh, no, Ma'am, you have* *to be accompanied...the rules...*And so, reluctantly, Marina had followed three elderly couples and a guide in a pink cashmere twin-set and a strand of glowing pearls, her old-money voice crooning *such generous philanthropy, visionary genius, acoustical perfection*, sweeping them through the history – the years of building and restoration, the number of performances each year, the number of seats in the three magnificent concert halls, the 130-something steps to reach the top balcony – until Marina had wanted to scream at all the facts and figures, at the cashmered refinement and pearly cultivation. Then, leading them on through passage after passageway, insisting they admire all the portraits on the walls: divas and folk stars, rock stars, pianists, cellists, jazz musicians, choirs...impossible to take them all in. And then Marina had seen it, an image from Australia: that familiar horsey face and massive jaw. And she'd remembered – how could she not – Connor's contempt for the Grand Dame of opera, his raging against a speech she'd made to a bunch of monarchists, complaining about being served at the post office by *some Indian or Chinese person*...as though they were all the same. Connor had refused to listen to her singing, ever again. *La Stupenda*, he'd said, *stupendously feckin' ignorant.* Marina remembered his every word. Was she destined to remember every word? Standing in that passageway, staring at fame, it had once again returned to her, as grief must return to everyone: unbidden.

She hauled herself up from the bed and went to the bathroom, looked sternly at her reflection. She must not succumb, must not fall into that deep dark well of self-pity. She must *soldier on*, as her father had instructed. Must remember, as her mother had insisted, how she had her *whole life* before her. A *whole life*: as though she hadn't been splintered into countless pieces, so many brutal shards. But her reflection told the story that her parents wanted: expressionless, featureless. Stoical.

Marina bent over the basin, splashed water on her face, thought about dinner and then didn't. Thought about emailing her sister, who'd asked if she'd met any *religious butters* in New York. Marina had smiled at the typo, at the thought of Christianity, yellow, thick and creamy, clogging up America. Or she could send the message to her neighbour back home. Edith Wilson, always *Mrs* Wilson, who'd told her that Connor's death had a purpose, that suffering was part of God's plan. Marina had wanted to shout into the woman's smug little face, at her Pollyanna-glad game, its cheap, phony, kick-up-your-heels attitude to life. She'd wanted to shout out what she knew in every bone, in every muscle and sinew of her body: that suffering was entirely arbitrary and always cruel. That it served no purpose at all.

Mrs Wilson, who had complained about the mess from their jacaranda tree and Connor had nodded as he listened. Asked if he should climb his ladder and glue every flower to the branches. Even now, Marina would look at that tree and hear his voice as he leaned on the fence, still see Mrs Wilson's indignant face, his crooked smile.

She missed that smile. That mouth. On her own mouth, on her breasts, and the way he used his tongue, caressed her.

She fell down on the bed again, stretched out her arms and legs, tried to loosen up. Then remembered she needed to set her alarm for a brisk, early start. Tomorrow she would sail past the Statue of Liberty and on to Ellis Island. As she punched in 7 am, Marina could picture the museum with its endless, grainy archival footage, the ubiquitous headphones, spools of recorded interviews, hundreds of objects: the worthy, futile attempt to recreate the past. But at least there wouldn't be too many people in this blistering cold…having to queue for a ferry in the open air, brave the choppy water. She wouldn't feel crowded, hemmed in, as she'd sometimes felt on their travels, people blocking her view of glorious paintings, treading on her toes, all that jostling in subways. At least she would have room to be alone.

She curled herself up on the bed and remembered a day in Florence. Walking inside the Duomo, when Connor had given her so many measurements her head was fit to burst: the size of the cathedral, the dimensions of its three huge bronze doors, the height of the arches in the aisles, the height of the dome itself. But she'd said nothing, indulged him as always. Until they'd stopped at a cafe for gelato, her first *real* gelato, divinely creamy pistachio, when he'd started reading aloud from his guidebook: all the ingredients and proportions and did she know what made it the best ice-cream in the world? It was the percentage of butterfat…and she'd lost it. Almost shouted. *For God's sake, Connor, just enjoy the bloody thing.*

She had lost her taste for ice-cream. She knew it would taste like regret.

She was prepared for the chilly wind blowing from the ocean but not for this endless, snaking queue. Packs of locals, judging by their accents and baseball caps; Scandinavians, predictably blonde and svelte; chattering Japanese, consulting guidebooks; Europeans or South Americans, speaking languages she couldn't locate. But she recognised the Italians: granite-faced men and glamorous women in tight jeans, leaning on the railing, taking up space in that Italian kind of way. But how much longer to wait? Marina huddled into the thick, heavy coat that she'd bought when she first arrived – and which she'd never need in Perth, with its temperate, kindly winters. It would be boiling at home right now, and so humid, so oppressive. Just before she'd left she'd heard the weather report, delivered in a howdy-doody voice: *The hottest year on record* and *one of our wettest Decembers…Folks, it looks like we're turning tropical!* As though they'd all be wearing hula skirts and slurping mangoes on the beach, instead of drowning or baking, dehydrating. Running out of life. It was hard to imagine the Australian heat on this glacial Saturday morning. Hard to imagine anything, really…going back to work, the dullness of her flat. But she knew for certain she wouldn't go back to study. Even though her sister had carefully raised the subject. Said it slanted; to the side.

'Off to see Liberty, then?'

A tall, smiling man with dark green eyes. She hadn't noticed him before.

'Of course,' she said. Then, hearing the snap in her voice: 'I'm going to Ellis Island as well. If this ferry ever leaves.'

'You sound like an Ossie,' he said.

Ossie, to rhyme with mossy: furry, green Australia.

He was delighted: Sydney three years ago…holiday… lovely people…Opera House…Marina wished the queue would start moving, stop this burst of breezy goodwill. He was Evan, by the way, and she was—? His smile widened even more.

'Ah, Marina,' he said, expansively. 'It means *of the ocean.* Did you know?'

She nodded, because she *did* know. Because Connor had told her.

'From a play by Shakespeare,' he said, 'and then given another life in one of my favourite poems.'

Marina startled. Because Connor had told her this as well, had given her the beauty of her name and her heart had opened up like a flower. And now, hearing this stranger, with his knowledge and dark green eyes and ridiculous smile reciting the words, stealing them – *let me resign my life for this life, my speech for that unspoken, the awakened, lips parted, the hope...*

'Please, stop,' she said. 'I know the poem, you don't have to—'

She saw his face drop. Heard him say sorry for being *so intrusive, so arrogant, for—* She held up her hand. This was even worse, she thought, this entanglement, his tangled up words of apology. She began to rummage in her bag for something, anything, and he drew away, put his hands on the railing and stared out to sea. She wanted none of this, standing in a queue in the meanness of the morning. Maybe she should walk back to the hotel, check in for an earlier flight, pack her bags...but she didn't have the energy. Going back seemed as hard as going forward.

The queue finally began to move; people were shuffling and she kept her distance, he kept his distance, and she was glad. Under shelter now, protected from the wind, as rucksacks were searched, bodies were patted by beefy security men. This time Marina didn't mind the wait. They could take hours if they needed to. She remembered her fears when Connor had hatched his New York plans. When

9

she'd dreamed of shopping mall massacres, bombs strapped to bodies or under cars, hooded figures with flick knives, and he'd given her the facts and statistics, of course: the radical decline in crimes against people and property, the heightened security at airports, in public buildings. *And you'll always be safe with me*, he'd said.

People were starting to scramble aboard and she followed, managed to find a seat at the end of a row, relieved to have given the talking man the slip. Relieved to be staring at the dull grey water, at skyscrapers in the distance, that world of bustle and money and purpose. She slowly removed her gloves, closed her eyes and gave herself up to the rocking of the ferry, let the words of passengers wash over her...*can't wait to see...massive...the torch and the flame...*the sounds of different accents and people being happy, just as she should be happy. *Swanning round New York*, someone at work had said, *half your bloody luck*. A cousin had said it differently: *It could have been worse, Marina; at least he left you comfortable.*

And then the feeling came over her again. The sharp and dark and dangerous thing, rocking to the waves and remembering the poem and the gift of her name, trying *not* to remember because all the details, every word and gesture, made him return to her, made him lost to her. When would she be done, would she ever be done, with this terrible ache inside her? She clenched her fists and told herself she would not cry. That she was on a mission. That he would have wanted her to be brave. If there had been time to tell her, this is what he would have said. But her breath was coming fast now and she knew she was weak and a coward and that she was nothing, nothing, without him. In this, too, she had failed him, she would always be failing him, sitting in a lecture room listening to important words, her phone switched off while his heart was giving way and she was much too late it would always be too late she would always be running to the hospital too late too late. *The two saddest words in the English language.* This, too, he had given her.

'Pardon me, Ma'am…Marina. Are you alright?'

She opened her eyes. It was the smiling man standing in front of her, his mouth now tight with concern. And because he'd asked her, because he'd seen something written on her face, because she felt so deeply, darkly lost, she told him she felt a little sea sick. He offered to squeeze in beside her, told her calmly to lean back, take deep breaths and think about *something pleasant.* She did as she was told, took those breaths, slowly, mindfully, and thought about Deborah. How they'd plaited each other's hair and told each other secrets and all the days at the beach, competing for the glossier tan. The sister who'd be waiting at the airport.

'Does that feel better?'

'Yes…yes, it does.' She looked at him, shyly. 'Thank you,' she said. 'And it's not even rough today.'

'I've been over on some blustery days,' he said, 'when people were really—' He bit his lip. 'Sorry, you didn't need to hear that.'

She gave him a smile. She owed him that much, at least, and some courtesy. A fragment of conversation. He was from Boston, he told her, and this was his seventh trip to Ellis Island. His great-great-great grandfather had arrived there in the 1890s, from Lithuania. And what had prompted *her* visit? Because the Statue of Liberty was the star attraction, but an immigration-processing centre – it didn't exactly pull in the crowds.

'My husband,' she said. 'He...couldn't make the trip but he really wanted me to go.'

She saw the man, Evan, look down at her hand, at her wedding ring.

'My wife,' he said slowly. 'We used to go travelling a lot, but we disagreed about everything along the way. Where to stay and what to see and politics – the way of the world.' He shrugged. 'I finally lost her in a Moscow market.'

'*Lost* her?'

'At the dancing bears enclosure. You might have seen the photos, where they chain up these poor enormous bears and make them learn stupid tricks.'

'You mean—' Marina was horrified.

'Oh, no, not that.' He laughed. 'She didn't get mauled to death. I just embarrassed her. Deeply.'

Marina raised an eyebrow.

'I stood at the fence,' he said, 'watching those miserable creatures, it was heartbreaking, I tell you. And the man who was with them, *training them*, well, I gave him a lecture, in English of course but he got my drift because he was shaking his fists at me, shouting at me, and Cindy started shouting at me, too. Told me to stop being such an idiot, to stop being so bossy. That was her actual word. *Bossy*.'

He gave her a rueful grin.

'So that's when I really understood,' he said. 'That it was over.'

He had what she imagined was a Boston voice: vaguely English. She looked at him more closely. He was maybe thirty, thirty-five, with crinkles round his eyes, a mouth that turned up at the corners.

'Did you have any children?' she said.

He shook his head. 'It was better that way.'

She recognised something in his voice; something he didn't say.

'We didn't have children either,' she said.

'Didn't? I thought—'

'My husband is dead.' She blushed. For her lie. For her foolishness.

'So, how long…I mean…'

'Two years.' She looked down at the floor. 'I should be—'

'You shouldn't be anything,' he said.

They were silent now, gently swaying to the lapping of the waves, and she felt the warmth of his coat beside her, felt lulled by the quiet drone of the ferry. She was looser, lighter, trying not to think, and it was peaceful, like the calmness of his voice when he'd told her to take deep breaths. And then, in a flash, she heard rousing shouts, a swell of gasps, people rushing to windows. *Look, there she is! Oh my god… awesome!* Marina looked out to see the statue getting closer. A shadowy green monument, alone in a desolate sea. Its presence seemed to fill the sky and, as the ferry drew near, Marina peered through the window, looked up and up and up. She saw the colossal sweep of an arm, the torch and the flame, the spikes of a crown. A face that gazed outwards, both strong and serene. The face of justice, Connor would have called it, and he would surely have been moved, just as she tried to be moved by this towering symbol of freedom, this beacon for the huddled masses, wasn't it? The tired, the hungry, the poor? But she couldn't feel it, looking up at this *thing* in the ocean; it was simply a very large statue, banally iconic.

Evan nudged her lightly, asked if she'd like to disembark.

She shook her head. 'It's too much for me,' she said. 'It's beyond human scale.'

'I've never been keen on her, either,' he said, out of the side of his mouth. 'Which is pretty un-American.'

She smiled at him. Properly this time. They watched the scores of people streaming off the ferry, some with cameras poised, others flapping their arms in the cold.

'Mind you,' he said, 'Ellis Island can be overwhelming, too. There are so many stories to listen to, so much to see. The numbers alone are staggering. Did you know that over twelve million people arrived there in the course of fifty years? And in one year alone, one million people. In one *day* alone, more than eight thousand.'

Marina was speechless. At this Connor and not-Connor. With his high cheekbones and flaring nose. Lithuanian, perhaps.

'Can you imagine?' he said. 'All those people…'

'I can't imagine. They're just numbers to me.'

He looked slightly stung.

'You sound like my wife,' he said. 'She got fed up with all my facts and figures. But I'm a history teacher, you see, so—'

'I'm not your wife,' she said. Snapped at him again. 'I just meant that the numbers don't help me to see.'

'I'm sorry…I didn't mean to—'

She softened. 'You keep saying sorry,' she said. 'Please don't.'

They looked at one another, unflinching. She felt that something had been settled between them.

The ferry was starting up again, leaving behind the climbers, the Liberty lovers, and they both lurched forward in their seats.

'Shall I try again?' he said. 'Give you some numbers that might help make it real?'

And so he told her about the voyage out. Up to 2000 people in an iron-hulled steam ship. Ten per cent of passengers died on the way, roughly 200 people per single boat. So those numbers tell a story, he said. Of sickness, disease, starvation. And don't get him started on the shipping companies who made obscene amounts of dollars from this trade in human need.

'So this is what you give your students?' she said. 'Do they take it in?'

'Some of them are interested,' he said. 'Well, as long as I do a PowerPoint or show some videos. But I like to tell them stories, too, and details. Sometimes it's the smallest things.'

'Like what? Tell me.'

He leaned back in his seat. 'One of the first things you'll see on the island is an object,' he said. 'A hook. A button-hook, to be precise. When the immigrants first arrived, they had to be inspected for illness and disease, so they wouldn't be a problem. An economic burden. The doctors—' He stopped, started again. 'The doctors would check for trachoma by turning the inner eyelid inside out with this sharp, cruel implement. They were the most feared people on the island.'

She felt the urge to take his hand, but instead she drew herself up, folded her own hands in her lap.

'I think—forgive me.' His voice was faltering now. 'I think I might have upset you.'

She shook her head. 'It's alright,' she said. 'Sometimes you need something small to help you see something so big.'

She didn't say, she wanted to say: and I have already faced the worst. And what I have faced is nothing, and it is everything. It is nothing.

He inclined his head towards her, making a space for them to share, as though they were the only two people on this sturdy boat, on their way to Ellis Island. And it pleased her, this space. It gave her some comfort. She wanted to hear his voice again, which was soft and deep, not Connor's voice, not his Irish lilt, slightly high-pitched.

'And the people who failed the test?' she said. 'I guess they were sent back to where they came from.'

He nodded. 'And it could happen so quickly,' he said. 'An inspector would, say, watch an immigrant walking up the stairs and would know straight away there was something wrong. It could take just seconds. Weeks and months to get here, and it was all over in seconds.'

Marina looked down at his hands and saw the raggedness of his fingernails, rough-edged and bitten, almost down to the quick. It made him seem so vulnerable, despite his sunny smile, his confident manner. It made him look lonely. She remembered the hook and the bears and the wife who called him bossy and she wanted to turn to him, tell him that none of this was fair. That he, her Connor, had suffered and she had not been there to help him. Was this the cruellest form of suffering? To die without the presence of love?

'The other thing I tell my students...' Evan's voice, returning her. 'Life for the immigrants was often very hard. Appalling conditions in factories and on farms, high infant-mortality rates, low life expectancy. Great unkindness. It's important to deal with the facts, not the rhetoric. All that stuff about America embracing the huddled masses.'

'The tired, the hungry, the poor,' she said. 'It's stirring stuff, isn't it?'

'And mostly bullshit,' he said. 'And I won't say sorry for that word.'

He was smiling but she saw the passion in his eyes, those dark green eyes that kept drawing you back, drawing her back. Connor's eyes were blue, blue Irish eyes, just like the song: *When Irish eyes are smiling, all the world seems bright and gay; a pile of sentimental shite*, he'd said.

'But what I want you to know—' Evan was watching her steadily. 'I keep making this journey because it's also a story of hope. It's my family and all the other families, all the young people who came here on their own: all of them with hope in their hearts. Even on those terrible boats, they did what people often do in times of great distress. They sang, they danced, they played cards. And they talked. To hear their own language. To remind themselves they were human. To—' He rubbed his head. 'I'm doing it again, aren't I? I've been doing it since we set sail. Chewing your ear off. Isn't that what they say in Australia?'

'Or talking the hind legs off a donkey,' she said. 'My grandpa said that all the time when I was a child. I used to think that donkeys walked by doing handstands.'

He laughed. 'Well, thanks for letting me lecture you,' he said. 'You've been, well, very indulgent. And I promise to leave you in peace once we get to the island. It's a place that asks us to be silent.'

It was a signal, she thought, an ending, and she didn't want this to end. She wanted him to talk, and to talk to him. After days in New York of hardly saying a word beyond the basics: *please, thank you, excuse me, how much.*

He gave her another one of his wide, American grins. 'Before you go,' he said, 'will you tell me what you do? You know, for a living. I'd kind of like to know.'

'I work in a shop,' she said. 'A music shop. Selling mostly rubbish.' *So now you know,* she thought, you kind of know. And should I tell you, too, how Connor was so proud of me, winning a prize at uni, telling everyone he met that I was taking on the world? Should I tell you that we'd talked of having children? Should I tell you how much he believed in me, and what we were making together?

They were married for seven years. He was forty-nine when he died, and she was twenty-eight. These numbers she would always remember.

As she picked up her gloves, preparing to disembark, she saw the glint of her wedding band, golden in the light.

'I'd started a degree,' she said. 'Hoping to become a lawyer. Only not the kind that makes a lot of money.'

She thought he might laugh but he didn't.

'I stopped,' she said. 'The truth is, I gave up.'

She waited for him to speak, having no idea of what he might say, what she wanted him to say. She could almost feel his heart beating under his coat, his thick, heavy coat that could never really shelter you, no matter how thick, no matter how heavy, from the need to feel blessedly alive. This patient, generous, honourable man. She thought she might weep with his goodness.

'But now…I think I might go back to it,' she said. 'The study.'

She hadn't known this until she said it.

She saw those bitten nails again and reached out her hand, entwined her fingers through his. Ah, the warmth.

She breathed it in: this ordinary, necessary gesture, of skin against skin. She felt the quiet pressure of his hand, could sense him watching her closely, and she knew she wanted to thank him. Give him something in return.

'Tell me about your great-great grandfather,' she said. 'Or did I leave out one of the *greats*?'

'I'd rather talk about you,' he said. 'Will you tell me more about you?'

She flushed. 'I don't think—not now…not at this moment.'

She made herself look into his eyes, remembering his stories, the larger sweep of history into which he was born, and which carried him to safety, would always carry him to safety. She knew she needed to begin.

'When I'm back in Australia…' She felt her heart knocking in her chest. 'You can call me…if you like.'

She disengaged her hand, watched her fingers tremble as she opened her bag, searched for her phone. Because she could never remember her number even though she'd tried over and over again to learn it off by heart.

'I would like that very much,' he said, quietly. Solemnly. 'Across the ocean. Marina.'

A Blast of a Poem

*Birds do it, bees do it, even educated fleas do it...*It was one of my mother's jaunty numbers as she whisked about with a duster. There were creamy songs as well, about moons and stars and rivers, and one that made me shiver without knowing why: *Do do that voodoo that you do so well.* But when she dusted my mother always wore a hairnet, and as a child this always made me sad. And once, I remember, when I begged her to release her golden tresses and try to look like a princess, she simply flicked me away. *Chimpanzees in the zoos do it, some courageous kangaroos do it.* She didn't miss a beat.

When I was fourteen years old and gushingly romantic, I asked my mother to tell me how they'd met: she and my long-dead father. It was on a train, she said; she was reading a book. He'd tapped her on the arm, pointed to a herd of cows outside the window and told her how to count them in a hurry: add up all their legs and divide by four. *A bit of a dasher*, she called him, *with a roguish smile like a film star.* Then she sighed heavily. *It could have been a riddle*, she said, *but he didn't think to ask me.*

When I was twenty-one, my mother came home tipsy from some outing. She whirled into the kitchen and turned in giddy circles, her dress a crimson swirl as she panted to a halt. *Such a good dancer, your father was*, she said. *He knew how to hold a woman, knew how to glide.* Then she leaned on the bench top and glared into my face. *But hopeless in bed*, she snapped. *A taker, always a taker. He never even kissed me.*

And now, when I recall that moment, I'm sorry I didn't ask her. Not then, not ever. Tell me mother, about your silent longing, the yearning of your body in the stillness of the night.

When I was twenty-four and my heart was shattered, I fell into my mother's arms. He was having sex with my best friend: a double and dismal betrayal. My mother could have said *plenty more fish in the sea* or *better to know sooner than later* but instead she held me close and slowly stroked my hair. I remember the gentle rhythm of her hand and the loving scent of her, like violets, and how, when I couldn't stop sobbing, she finally pulled away from me and looked me sternly in the eye. *Fidelity*, she said. *It's not all it's cracked up to be.*

When I first slept with Ollie, I laid down my rule. No sex with anyone else. *Sex is a humanly specific activity*, I said, *and I want you to honour my human specificity* (I remember it so clearly: twenty-nine and bookish, sprouting my textbook words). He laughed and nuzzled my neck. *And another thing*, I said (I was, in those days, what a friend called *statuesque*, with unfashionable curves and a full ripe mouth), *I want you to listen to what I like and I want you to do more than tweak my nipples and then poke yourself inside me.*

Bloody hell, he said. *Is this where feminism has brought us?*

I knew at once that he was joking.

How did I know that I *loved* him? It took me less than a week. He asked me what I liked and he knew without asking about all the other things I liked, and he never once poked. He took his time, made himself wait, made me wait, entered me and found me, lost me, lost himself, and I didn't know where I ended and he began. But it was the poem that really clinched it. I rapped on his door, aching for sex, and he waved at me, book in hand, from the sofa, asked me to sit down and listen. *It's a poem about cows*, he said, *I mean, who would have thought*, spilling out words about a great fat tongue and sweeping lashes, an udder splayed richly on the green, and his eyes were shining and *isn't it a blast*, he said. I was straight away undone. *I love you*, I said, and he wrapped me up and told me that he loved my great fat tongue and my sweeping lashes and my voluptuous udders splayed richly on his chest, and we laughed and made love and made many sodden promises.

But in the dark of night I remembered my mother. The cows in the field and the film-star smile and the book she should have kept reading.

I was four years old when my father died, and all I remember is a very shiny forehead, and a pair of legs behind a newspaper, with some cigarette smoke drifting in the air.

My mother told me I was very lucky to have found a man like Oliver. *Kind*, she called him. *He listens to you. And he knows how to have a laugh.* It was the closest she came to expounding a philosophy of love: how you could be sitting on a train and meet a man who could have been another kind of man but wasn't.

She never re-married. She never even brought a man home. She did go dancing for years at the Embassy Ballroom with *a dear old codger* named Frank. She'd met him at her tenpin bowling club and his forte was Latin American. There was also a retired teacher who took her to see foreign films, although she seemed to like the choc bombs best of all. But as far as I could tell there was never any sex: there were no coy smiles or innuendoes, no transfiguring glow. It was Oliver, after all, who claimed her heart, who made her giggle like a smitten young girl.

And how did I know that I loved him even more? We were weeding in the back garden, grunting and complaining, blaming ourselves for being so busy at work and too dog-tired on weekends and *now look*, I said, *all these bloody weeds, we'll never be done.* He stood up straight and pulled back his hat, squinting in the harsh morning light. And then he asked me in a very quiet voice − I can still hear the tremor − *Are you…pregnant? Because your belly suddenly seems*—

Fat, you mean, I said, ready to rebuke, lecture, sulk, but he moved towards me and folded me up, kissed me on the cheek. *Would you like to make a baby?* he said. This man who'd never held a baby in his life. And I gasped and nodded and he cupped my bum and said that he was worried: how with my very juicy arse and his very skinny legs, our baby might never stand up.

I went off the pill and the sex was even better. Through-the-roof orgasmic. *It's something primal*, I told him, *like this is what my body is meant for.* He teased me, said I sounded like Sigmund Freud. But *he* felt it, too, wanting to come into me so deeply, make a life inside me. *Our life. I just want more of us*, he said. I began to dream in pictures, ones I remembered from an old school text: a sweetly alien creature, thumb in mouth, its head much too big for its body; a pair of floating starfish hands. And then my own proud hand on my rounded belly, encountering the world. I began to notice babies: unknown ones in prams, whose arms flapped about like wind-up toys; babies peering over shoulders; wide eyes and chortles and spikes of hair glowing in the sun. I held the babies of friends, breathed in their milky scent and stroked their flawless skin, trembled at their tininess. Ollie noticed, too, and held these creatures in unsteady arms, until he settled into them, soon began to coo at them, sing to them, soothe their howls of distress. *Did you see?* he would say to me later. *Those eyelashes, as thick as brooms.* Or *those fat legs like sausages.* Or, *did you see how he chomped on my finger, as if his life depended on it?* We saw scrumptious babies, cheeky babies, very ugly babies, and *what if we had a very ugly baby*, he laughed, *we'd see it on people's faces.* And then he pressed against me. *I want to make a beautiful baby*, he said, *one with your violet eyes and pneumatic lips and everything about you.*

They say to give it a year before you need to be concerned. They say. The books were bristling with advice. Check the ovulation cycle. Take your temperature. Eat plenty of greens. Try yoga. Swimming; it's meant to loosen something or other. And so we finally had the tests and there was nothing *wrong* with us at all. Ollie's cousin suggested a holiday, away from the humdrum and familiar: *That's how Lisa and I got pregnant*, he said, puffing out his chest. *You mean <u>Lisa</u> got pregnant*, I said to Ollie. *What is it with men these days?* But we followed his advice and took a few weeks' leave and travelled to places that neither of us had been to. We saw the Coliseum and the Spanish Steps and the sad, narrow bed in which Keats had languished and died. We saw the Freud Museum and the church of fifty-four hearts. We had sex in shabby hotels and apartments with rusty water, in beds with sagging mattresses that made us roll into the middle. We never argued. We held hands across restaurant tables as we talked. He liked Bella for a girl, and Catherine. *Classical*, he said. And Joe for a boy, or Adam, *what did I think of Adam?* But boy or girl, he didn't mind at all, *as long as it's healthy*. I'd scoffed at him, told him that's what everyone says. The useless things people say.

When I hit thirty-five, I asked my mother if she'd ever wanted another child. She looked up from her sewing, said it would have been *nice* for me to have a sibling. Then she looked down again, peering closely at her needle. *But I didn't want to…you know*, she said. *Anymore*. That weekend, I told her we were trying for a baby. She was tearily thrilled and mightily relieved to know I wasn't *that kind of woman. Who thinks children will interfere with her lifestyle*. She said the word *lifestyle* as though she'd just seen something nasty in the bottom of her glass. We were sitting in our back garden and the sky was piercing blue and there were no more weeds and there was new brick paving and carefully tended plants in cheery red pots. My mother drank beer and I drank water and I remember how the blue of the sky, dotted with fluffy clouds, convinced me that all would be well.

We kept on trying. We kept on talking. *It'll happen soon. Don't worry. We've got plenty of time. No earthly reason. Just relax*, our friends began to chorus, the ones with fuzzy-haired, gurgling babies and dimpled toddlers. One of those dimpled toddlers had a contract with a modelling agency and Ollie called this *child abuse*. We stopped seeing those friends but we didn't stop seeing all the others. *Relax* was what my GP said as well, what the expert on the radio said. I tried different kinds of herbal tea and St John's Wort, also known as chase-devil. We did a course in meditation, where Ollie always fell asleep. I tried not to look in shops at jumpsuits and bonnets and snug woollen booties, and he stopped suggesting names. I tried not to hate a diminutive friend who even on the verge of giving birth hardly made a blip in the universe.

And so we made a kind of mantra, Ollie and I. *Are you OK?* one of us would say to the other. Sitting on the sofa watching TV. Texting on the way to work. At parties, wandering into different rooms and then finding each other again. Brushing a hand. Stroking a cheek. And once, I remember so clearly, Ollie called it *an ego thing. You know, just wanting to replicate your own miserable self.* He must have seen the look on my face because he flushed very red and asked me to forgive him in that low, quiet voice that always tells me I have touched something deep inside him. We curved our bodies together and held each other close. *Are you OK?* he said. I didn't tell him, I never told him, how I sometimes screamed at the sight of my menstrual blood. How I gazed at babies in shops, talked to them, patted them, until mothers edged away from the slightly crazy lady. How I sometimes sat in a chair staring at unyielding walls. Or how, just once, I stripped in front of a mirror and plunged my fingernails deep into my flesh.

My mother and our friends knew to stop asking. For that, at least, I was grateful.

And then one night I woke to find an empty space beside me, groped my way dopily to find him. He was hunched over his computer and when he turned to face me, his eyes were wet with tears. *It's my fault*, he said, *all my bloody fault.* He'd been reading all about it on the net, *years of cigarettes and too much booze and even though the tests said...I've let you down so badly and I'm such a useless fuck.* I could have said *it's no one's fault* or *you mustn't even think that* but instead I cupped his face and told him he was all I ever wanted. Needed. Craved for.

When you touch me, he said, *I feel so much at peace*.

And as the weeks became months and the months became years, my life began to feel like an old-time movie, in which the leaves of a calendar are ripped off and tossed aside by some cruel, invisible hand. At some point I must have stopped rubbing my belly, as if trying to comfort someone. He must have stopped saying *Tonight's the night, for sure*. And we must have decided, without talking about it, not to talk about it anymore.

At my mother's seventieth birthday party, when Ollie and I were fifty, I saw him hoist someone's tiny child onto his lap and listen to her babbling. I stood at a doorway, watching: the way the child's feet dangled in the air; her look of fierce concentration. Ollie's arm around her waist; his steady, patient breathing; his nodding in time to words I couldn't hear. He glanced up and caught my eye and I saw such softness, such tenderness, in his face. For the child or for me, it was impossible to tell.

And that night, when he entered my body, he kissed me on the forehead and told me I was all he needed. *Forever.* And when I came, slow and dreamy, safe in his arms, he couldn't stop laughing. *You made a mooing noise*, he said. *You've never done that before.*

I remembered the great fat tongue and the giant udders and telling him I loved him as he sprawled on the sofa with his blast of a poem. And so I wrapped my arms around him and mooed again, loudly, playfully, stupidly, to stop myself from washing him with tears.

Feet to the Stars

A week back at school and it felt like he'd never left. And so many new students, blurring into Holly, Molly and Polly. The calendar already crammed with staff meetings, parent-teacher evenings, wine-and-cheese evenings, the athletics carnival, the swimming carnival. And now a Year 10 camp at Dwellingup. He'd always loathed school camps, with their calculated bonding games, artificial problem-solving, spurious trust exercises. Jolly nature rambles. Six years of university, from Beowulf to Virginia Woolf, and they expected him to surge through oceans, climb ragged peaks, brave the flying fox. Was the phys. ed. staff required to teach the formal complexities of the sonnet? Discuss what was free about free verse? Leave others to commune with bloody nature, he thought, and bury their bodily waste in the dirt. Leave others to endure four whole days and three long nights without the solace of whisky or wine.

Oh, he'd heard the argument many times: camps build resilience, resourcefulness, a sense of independence in the girls. Well, yes, until they retreated to their modish homes with security intercoms, behind towering fences with iron railings. To their rooms graced with every technological apparatus known to humankind, and serviced every week by a cleaner. To mothers perched aloft in their four-wheel drives, who ferried their charges to school in the morning and picked them up promptly at 3.45.

Paul looked at his watch. Ten more minutes until the final bell.

Maybe ten more years until retirement?

He'd be glad to get home, taste that first slug of alcohol. Not that his flat was *home*: more a place to mark truckloads of essays and watch TV. He hardly had the energy to read these days. He turned the corner, left onto the highway, left again at the roundabout. No matter how hard he tried to resist he always slowed down to look, still ambushed by the bright red door that Lydia had painted when they'd first moved in. *A renovator's dream*: meaning slack or incompetent tradies, DIY disasters. And then after the children came along, all the extensions, the modern touches: four double bedrooms, a marble bathroom with a spa, a pristine white kitchen, a gazebo, a swimming pool no one ever swam in. The years they'd spent planning, shopping for the perfect tiles, the perfect floor rugs and window treatments. It had given them something to contemplate: items to ponder, feelings to avoid, during thirty years of marriage. Plenty of time to fall out of love: you fell in, and then you fell out, your heart an obedient muscle, learning to contract.

He hadn't tried to explain this to his sister, whose heart was full of love for the church. And what could he have said to his daughters? The corrosive silences? The lonely marriage bed? You couldn't say that to your children, to anyone, really, and so he'd said nothing, or muttered it was *all for the best*. At least his parents weren't alive to hear the news. His mother would have wrung her hands; his father would have snarled about *people chucking it in, no stickability these days*. His parents were married for forty years and he never saw them touch, except on the day Aunty Elsie died and his mother had cried on his father's shoulder.

Paul thought about ducking into the supermarket for some eggs, or maybe he could pick up another takeaway pizza. *No anchovies, thanks*: it had become his signature tune. He'd always been a lousy cook, or maybe he'd just been lazy. The cooking had always been Lydia's job and she'd always done it superbly. The virtual banquets when they *entertained*: spending hours in the kitchen, setting the table, placing glasses, napkins and flowers *just so*. Always a stickler for the niceties. But at least she'd had the courage to finally make a move. She'd been able to imagine something different, maybe something better: a new job as a curator, overseas travel, and a new *vibrant lifestyle*, she called it, in Northbridge. *Just a stroll from the cafes and restaurants and the art-house cinema*. Sounding like a glossy brochure. And did people actually *stroll* these days, Paul wondered. Like latter-day flâneurs?

He remembered Lydia standing at the front door, jangling her keys in that way she had, the sound of a busy woman. How she'd made him look away from the TV screen and declared that they *couldn't go on this way*. And later, she'd *arranged things* as well: the sale of the house, furniture, books, the packing up; packing up decades, trundling them away. There was just one moment when she'd suddenly seemed real to him, when she'd looked at him across the breakfast table and told him there wasn't anyone else, that she'd always been faithful. How she wanted him to know that. *As I've been to you*, he'd said. And maybe that was something, after all, to have kept some kind of faith. Or would an affair or two have helped them, spiced things up? How would he know? How would he know what worked? *Follow your heart*, isn't that what people said? A slogan to frame and hang on your wall. *Live the life you have imagined.* He'd once seen those words on a T-shirt hanging in a window, with no attribution of the source. It was Henry David Thoreau, who'd lived by a lake in contemplative solitude, and extolled the virtues of self-reliance and back-to-nature simplicity. Paul had wanted to march into the shop and announce that the T-shirt was a big fat lie. That Thoreau's mother had made his dinner every night and taken it to his contemplative house by the contemplative lake. But you couldn't fit that on a T-shirt, could you?

Paul loosened his tie, tried not to think about the heat. The school had a new state-of-the-art science block and a Performing Arts Centre with more seats than the MCG, but no air con for the English classrooms. Suffering for art again. Friday, last period, and he'd given the girls twenty minutes to write their thoughts on the representation of infanticide in *Medea*. Given himself a break as well. Until Emerald asked him how you spelt *infanticide* and *what's the word for that Jason guy, the one that sounds like a dip...hummus?* Hubris, he reminded her. Emerald wasn't too bright but she was sweet, and sweetness was welcome on a sagging Friday with another dull weekend ahead of him. The usual dinner with his sister and her docile husband and dull kids. Maybe a catch-up dinner with his daughters, who'd say they'd get back to him, as usual. A drink with Henry, who would moan about one of his two ex-wives, especially the one who was threatening to cut off his access because he'd let his daughter watch an MA movie.

Henry had told him about the research: how men thought about sex every fifteen seconds.

Paul loosened his tie a little more. It had been three years since the divorce. Maybe seven years since he'd made love. Not long after Lydia (*after Lydia*, his life thus defined), Henry had encouraged him to try dating again. It had taken him a year to give it a go, dip his toes in the water; nothing to lose, after all – at least that was what he tried to tell himself each time he fronted up to a restaurant or bar. Four different dates in all, ranging from the mildly dispiriting to the profoundly depressing. His own performance, though, had been admirably consistent: tongue-tied, blushing, as gauche as a teenage boy. He concluded that he'd lost the knack, or the heart.

He looked at the rows in front of him, at those courteous, compliant, mostly hard-working girls. How would *they* spend their weekend? Study and homework, of course, but he'd heard the gossip in the staff room about binge drinking, uppers and downers, sex. (Oral sex was all the rage, apparently, because a girl could maintain her virginity.) But weekends might be difficult for badly acned Helena, sitting in the front row, whose father had told him it was just as well his girl had brains *cos she sure ain't much of a looker.* Or for Billie, who always wore a jumper, even in heatwaves, to cover up the cuts on her wrists. He'd taken her aside, tried to talk with her, and she'd never once met his eye. And next to her, Chloe, who had openly declared her attraction to girls. This morning he'd stood at the top of the stairs to hear Genevieve Tate call out to her: *Loser lezzo.* Another voice had called back: *You're such an arsehole, Gen, an ignorant arsehole.* He couldn't have put it better himself. But today there was no Eleanor; she hadn't been to class for a week. Nell: the girl who was always immaculately prepared for lessons, alarmingly keen to excel. With her stick-thin limbs and tell-tale lollipop head. Smart and engaged and his very favourite student, when you weren't supposed to have one.

Imogen shot up her hand with that bizarre salute of hers, an eager Dr Strangelove, asked about the assessment next week. Could they have extra time because the ball was coming up and they had a maths test as well and physics the week after and suddenly there was a chorus of complaint, *too many tests, just not fair, no one understands.* He told them they'd just have to organise their time but their voices were getting louder, more insistent, braying at him as if the whole damned world was conspiring against them and before he could stop himself he shouted, told them *to get a grip, get a sense of* – he swallowed the word *fucking* – *perspective.* He could see twenty shocked faces staring at him. He'd never shouted at his students before, in countless years of teaching, and he'd been only one word away from an official reprimand. The bell rang and he dismissed them, watched them scuttle from the room, peering at him through the big glass walls. (He could hear them already: *Mr H. was, like, acting really weird.*)

The note on his desk looked startled, written in large, upright words. *The boss* wanted to see him, straight after school. The principal. Mrs Taylor. Did anyone know her first name? She reduced all the teachers to stammering stone-age idiots whenever she asked them a question. Even the burly gardener Alf cleared off when he saw her coming. And *straight after school*? What had he done wrong? He was feeling even more nervous when Marie ushered him in (looking, as always, as if she knew that something grave, if not downright catastrophic, was about to descend on the school).

The principal rose from behind her desk and gave him a practiced smile. He'd never been in her office before; it was as big as a ballroom, with jarrah panels and a thick beige carpet with the triumphant school crest bang in the middle; velvet chairs; a painting that looked like a Drysdale, probably *was* a Drysdale. The principal thanked him for coming at such short notice, gestured for him to sit down (on burgundy velvet) and more or less commanded him to admire the river view.

'And so, Mr Harford,' she said briskly, 'we have a problem on our hands; a sad state of affairs, really. I'm hoping you will help us.'

She told him about Eleanor. Who had developed an eating disorder, but of course he must know this, or have guessed. Who was in a private clinic, broken down, just broken. Paul nodded and said he'd been aware, that it was hard not to notice.

Nell. She was sixteen years old.

'She asked to see you,' said the principal. She told him how *the poor girl* didn't want any other visitors except a sister

34

she was very close to. She didn't even want her parents to come, although of course they were fully entitled. Had been visiting regardless. And something in the set of the principal's mouth told Paul something about the parents.

'You see, Mr Harford,' she said, 'Eleanor thinks very highly of you. She says you've been kind to her.'

He searched his memory, puzzled, and she leaned forward slightly.

'Sometimes it's just a word here or there,' she said. 'A comment on an essay. We don't always know, do we?'

She asked him if he'd be good enough to consider it. Of course, he said, as if he'd just agreed to open a jar of pickles for her. She told him that the parents had agreed, and that Marie would give him the appropriate file, *highly confidential, you understand.* But now, as he was beginning to feel the weight of what she'd charged him with, he told her he wasn't sure what to say.

'Listening is a good strategy,' she said calmly. 'But I'm sure you know that, as a teacher. And as a parent. You have children, do you not, Mr Harford?'

'Two daughters, yes.'

She shook her head, picked up her cup.

'They seem so confident these days, don't they?' she said, and took a sip of tea. 'The girls. *Out there,* isn't that the expression? But being young, it never changes, really. It never gets any easier.'

She set down her cup and rose from her chair. Paul took his cue and rose as well, not sure what to do with his hands, or his feet for that matter. Was he meant to keep two paces behind? Open the door for himself? But the principal was holding out her hand again and thanking him, asking to be kept informed, and her grasp was firm, friendly. She opened the door and held him with a look.

'I have two daughters as well,' she said. 'They can be—well, let's just say I was relieved when they finally left home.'

Paul quietly closed the door behind him, flummoxed, and Marie looked up from behind her gleaming jarrah desk. Her hair was stiff like his mother's used to be, sprayed into submission with lacquer from a can. It gave off a pungent, metallic smell.

'I've met one of them,' she whispered. 'One of the daughters.' She darted a sympathetic look at the principal's door.

So it seemed he'd been kind and must take his kindness to a clinic. Try to help a young woman he hardly knew, and whose uniform hung on the body of a child. He'd already driven past the place where she was being treated, seen the carefully clipped garden where maybe they would sit together, where he would try to listen to an anorexic girl who looked in a mirror and saw obscene rolls of fat. Body dysmorphic disorder. Those pages in her file, where she'd been diagnosed, categorised: a special, common case.

He parked his car and entered the building through smoothly gliding doors. There were cream leather sofas and cheerful cushions in the reception room; a neat stack of shiny *National Geographic*s; and on the walls, consoling images of waterfalls and trees. The receptionist had cheekbones like knives, tight skin and tight smile, and her accent was French, maybe, something continental at any rate, and classy. And, yes, Eleanor was waiting and would he care to take a seat while she called her room? Paul sat, crossed his legs nervously. And here she was, straight away: Nell. Looking much younger than he remembered her, all bones, angles and knots, in a pale blue summer dress.

'Mr Harford, thank you for coming,' she said.

Like a poised hostess about to offer him a martini. She looked so unexpected, away from the classroom, even strange. She'd like to sit in the garden, if that was OK, and as they walked outside she lowered her head and told him in a whisper that men weren't allowed in her room, in any girl's room. No men except family, that is.

'It must be very sad sometimes, being a man,' she said. 'To always be the object of suspicion.'

And it struck him again: she was only sixteen years old.

They sat on the bench and he told her it was good to see her. That they all missed her in class.

'Ah, yes, discussions,' she said blankly.

Useless words were rattling through his head: this seems a nice place...*nice*...it feels good in the sun...how long do you think...how do you feel? How do you feel, Nell, sitting in the shade, poised and polite and so pitifully thin?

'My parents are mad at me,' she said, her voice still blank. 'Well, not *mad* mad; you know, not all red and shouting, but angry inside.' She looked up at him. 'I embarrass them. Being here.'

Again he could prattle on, chatter like an ape: I'm sure they love you very much...they just want the best for you... But she was changing direction, asking him about school. Which text were they doing now? How many assessments had she missed, Mr Harford, and, without thinking, he told her to call him Paul.

'That's a warm name,' she said, and he flinched. He'd never thought of this before: that she might have a crush on him. The kindly teacher; maybe the substitute father.

'Do you like your name?' she said. 'I don't like mine. My mother named me after her mother. She named me after a dead person.'

'Well, I hope—I'm sure she was a good person.'

'My mother says she was. She wanted me to grow up to be just like her.'

'But you didn't,' he said.

This seemed to release her, and her voice began to gather force. 'All my life, everyone's been on my case,' she said. 'You must do this, Eleanor, be that, don't do this, oh, no, you won't like that...Go to university, make up your mind; everyone else has...' She gave him a tiny smile. 'At the beginning of the year—' She stopped, started again. 'You asked me if I had any plans for when I left school and I said I didn't have a clue. And you told me that was wonderful. And you didn't go on and on about it, telling me I didn't have to make up my mind, I was still so young and I had my whole life before me blah di blah di blah...You said it like a poem instead.'

He told her she was his very best student but she shook her head, reminded him of her last essay, and bombing out in the exams. Her face had tightened again and she seemed to retreat into that deep, dark place which was only an idea to him. The dark isolation.

'Essays, exams,' he said. 'That's not what I mean by *very best*.'

She tilted her face to him and asked if he had any children. And did he wish he'd had a son? No, he said, no regrets.

'My parents wanted a son,' she said. 'I have two older sisters.'

She told him how they'd both *done so well*, like a proud parent, not a hint of irony in her voice. And how they both *look so good; you know, slim and gorgeous.* He was on the point of asking what they did, these slim and gorgeous high achievers – medicine or law, no doubt – and then he pulled himself up, because *doing* was part of the problem for Nell. She was off on another path now, asking about the girls and who was playing the lead in *Romeo and Juliet*, chatting, holding up her end of a conversation, holding herself up. But she was beginning to tire and the sun was getting hot and she said it was time to go. Fifteen minutes was her limit. Was that a rule, he wondered, or had she chosen it herself? He wanted to say: please go inside and eat, give yourself the nourishment you deserve, but he could hear himself sounding like a counsellor or a well-intentioned parent and he was neither of those things and she was thanking him for coming, Mr Harford. She'd rather call him Mr Harford, if that was OK, and would he please visit her again? And as they stood up together, she glanced at him shyly and told him he looked *kind of sad.*

'Sometimes you look hollowed out,' she said.

Paul was startled. And touched beyond imagining. By this child who had been watching him, taking care, when she could barely take care of herself. And then she sighed, seemed to throw a thought up in the air, tried to catch it as it fell. 'Someone in my therapy group,' she said, 'he feels better when he hugs trees. Have you ever hugged a tree?'

Paul shook my head.

'No, I can't see you doing that,' she said earnestly. 'It seems, I don't know…preposterous.'

And then she said goodbye and slipped away through those big glass doors. Back to her five-star hotel.

Wonderful, he'd said. Don't worry about a signed-on-the-dotted-line future. Was this the kindness he'd given her? This cheery, fatuous scrap?

He waited to be asked and, a fortnight later, made another visit. This time Nell was already waiting in the garden and he could see some colour in her cheeks. And she looked less knotted, a little calmer. She was watching him watching her and he suddenly felt wrong: he was a set of prying eyes like all the others. Nell laughed a little crookedly, and as they took their place on the bench, she told him she knew what he was thinking.

'I've put on some weight,' she said, matter of fact. 'Half a kilo exactly. They call it making progress.'

She had a splash of freckles across her nose. He'd never noticed them before.

'I need to tell you something; can I tell you something?' she said. 'About the man who cleans my room?'

Paul held his breath, but she didn't look frightened or repelled.

'I was sitting up in bed,' she said, 'and he stopped at the doorway and just kept looking and looking at me and' – her voice trembling now – 'he told me how I looked like his sister and she died from what I had, and then he…he just started to cry.' She reached out and took Paul's hand, warm in the morning sun. 'It was just these soft, quiet tears and he told me I didn't have to die. Then he turned around and walked away.'

Paul left a space; waited.

'I know I'm supposed to report him,' she said. 'But it... well, he just made me feel very sad because his sister died and because he cared about her.'

Paul heard what she wasn't saying: my parents don't really care about me; not in the way I want them to.

'He wanted to help you,' he said.

Nell nodded. She suddenly removed her hand and patted her head, asked him what he thought of her hair. 'My mother told me once that plaits are *childish*.'

'And what did you say to her?'

'Nothing. But I wanted to say, *get lost...get fucked*, actually.'

'Well, there's your answer.'

She looked at him wryly. 'The doctor told me to be honest,' she said. 'He didn't tell me to say *get fucked*. To my mother.' She looked up at the sky. 'Can you hear the birds?' she said. Sitting on a bench, with her schoolgirl plaits and thin summer dress, still so bony and frail. 'The woman who runs my group, she tells us to listen to the birds, to all the different kinds.'

'And do you?'

'Yeah. But they're just...well, different.'

She looked down at her lap, and then up into his eyes. She had dark green, almond-shaped eyes.

'Do you know what I like about books?' she said. 'Well, the ones we read, anyway. They don't give you answers.'

'You wrote that in your last essay,' he said. 'It's one of the most important things you'll ever learn.'

'You're very wise,' she said, and he told her, no, he was just a pompous prat. She laughed; it occurred to him he'd never heard her laugh before.

'And I like the way you always listen,' she said. 'Not just to the things we say but to the spaces; you know, what's in between. And I always like listening to you reading to the class. Your voice…it kind of blends into the words, so it's all about the words and not about you.'

He felt his face redden with embarrassment. Sitting with this damaged child and feeling blessed to be with her, a young woman who was almost certainly much stronger than she thought and who had everything she needed inside her.

'May I ask you a favour?' she said, and he nodded.

'I'd like to introduce you to my parents.'

'*Introduce* me?'

'When I leave, when I get out of here, I want you to come to dinner and—' She took a deep breath and he was anxious now. It was what he'd feared after all. 'Well, the truth is, I want you to meet my sister. Francesca. Frannie. She's a lot older than me and I know you're not married anymore and she's really beautiful, I mean not just to look at but as a person. And she's a really smart lawyer and she plays the flute like an angel and most of all she's just so kind and—'

She petered out, sat and waited, staring into his stunned face. He smiled stiffly, told her that she was the kindest person herself, to be thinking of him in this way.

'But I'm fifty-five years old,' he said quietly. 'Your sister won't—'

'No, no, she will, she'll just adore you. She's always telling me how she prefers older men and—'

He had to laugh. It was like hugging trees, he thought: you could do it in theory but you'd look bloody stupid if you were caught in the act. And *prefers older men*? What on earth would Nell know about that? Where did this come from? And then he saw her face: vexed, almost angry.

'I'm not laughing at you,' he said. 'I'm laughing at the idea.'

'What idea?'

'Of me with...the idea of...'

'Hope, you mean?'

He sighed. There was no way he could win this battle, if that's what they were doing here, and was winning the point, anyway? He tried to speak but Nell beat him to it.

'You adults are all the same,' she said wearily. 'People telling me I'm making progress and I have so much to look forward to and that life can be good if I just allow myself to...blah di blah di blah.' She looked at him sternly. 'And you're no different from the rest of them. Preaching all this stuff and not believing it yourself, not *doing* it yourself.'

He sat back. 'Nell, it's different for me. Look, I'm really touched by your gesture, your offer, it's very—'

'Sweet of me, I know.' She sighed. 'And then you'll tell me you're too old to start again and if that doesn't work you'll tell me you don't need a girlfriend or a wife or even love or whatever you want to call it because you have your work or your kids or some dumb hobby to give your life meaning. You see, Mr Harford' – smug now, triumphant – 'I've been in therapy for years.'

He folded his hands together, uselessly.

'So will you come to dinner?' she said.

She reminded him of his daughters as children, the power of their persistence. He weighed up what she'd said and resorted to the self-help mantra: what was the worst that could happen? A slightly awkward few hours? Public humiliation? Or maybe he could do a deal: he'd come to dinner if she promised to start eating. Properly. Or would that only make things worse?

'OK,' he said. 'I accept. But only if you promise to be there. And if you don't try to make me fall in love with your sister.'

Nell's face lit up, like a child excitedly clapping her hands. And then she stood up and shook his hand, sealed the deal, and asked him to visit in a week. He watched her walk away, this slip of a girl, this determined young woman who'd been thinking, she said. So she knew he wasn't married anymore. Maybe the whole class knew; all his students. Maybe he'd been the object of attention for a whole five minutes, before they'd returned to their iPods and iPads and tweets, the world of instant likes.

Sitting on the bench, hearing unknown birds, feeling the welcome sun on his face, he thought of a couple of friends who'd recently retired. One was going on a cruise with his bridge club; the other had taken up golf. Both possibilities appalled him. And then he remembered the evening he'd walked to the ocean and sat alone on the grassy bank. As he listened to the rolling, melancholy waves, he'd thought of Lydia. Wondered where she went in the middle of the night, and if she felt what he felt, beneath her vibrant new lifestyle, her stroll to the cinema and the cafes: the emptiness. Sitting on the shore, as the waves kept rolling in and breaking, rolling in, *like the thud of a great beast stamping*. Virginia Woolf. Every serious reader knew the end of her story: how she had put on her overcoat, filled its pockets with heavy stones and walked into water. It was a river, not an ocean, which had called her, but she had heard the great beast stamping.

And then he'd stood up from the bank and gone home.

❧

Lydia. He'd first seen her in a record store, pretending to browse through the albums, struck by the gold of her hair. She'd chosen a record and held it out, turned to him (those dark brown eyes and thick black lashes) and said dreamily, *Judy Collins, such purity in her voice.* And he'd pretended to know her, the singer. Agreed with Lydia's assessment. Somehow found the courage, his hands damp with fear, to ask her out. A Vietnam moratorium march of all things, the two of them chanting in the tidy streets of Perth, people gawking on the sidelines or jeering as they sang out their hymn: *One, two, three, four, we don't want your bloody war.* They had that much in common, he and Lydia, in the good old days: making love, not war.

And now, after all this time, the prospect of companionship. Maybe friendship. Something more. But he remembered his gray hair and crinkled face...*Crinkled?* Lined with age and worry, veritable chasms of loss. And he was only a teacher, after all, while she, Francesca, was a lawyer, probably a high-powered one, if she was as smart as Nell had declared. He pictured the dinner. It could be a mild form of torture, seeing the woman's indifference or, even worse, her contempt. And exactly how *young* was she, anyway? If Nell was seventeen, her sister could be twenty-five, maybe even thirty. Or maybe Nell was the child of a second marriage, in which case her sister could be older. Thirty-five? But that was still too many years between he and this female paragon. And what if she wanted children? Now that he'd come so far. Now that he was already thinking, in spite of himself, in terms of something more serious. More enduring.

He remembered what one of his teachers used to say, when he thought you were getting too full of yourself; when insult was the chief pedagogical mode: *pull your head in, son.* And he remembered his father's mocking words: *Wouldn't say boo to a goose.*

On Monday morning he woke from a comic-grotesque nightmare in which the lovely Francesca, who he'd imagined had long dark hair and an enigmatic smile, had thrown a bowl of oxtail soup in his face. *Oxtail soup?* Would French onion or cream-of-mushroom have made it any better?

He told himself it was just a dinner. He wasn't going down on bended knee, diamond ring in hand. But when he shaved he was forced to look in the mirror, had to turn away. Not wishing to reflect on his reflection.

At school the girls had made a card for Nell and asked him to sign it. One of those jumbo-sized cards, meant for celebrations and silly occasions, and at the top of the page a quotation in bright red letters: *Clownlike, happiest on your hands, feet to the stars.* Sylvia Plath. Bella said it had taken ages to find words that everyone agreed on: some girls just wanted a simple message like *get well soon* or *we miss you*, and the school sacristan preferred something from the Bible.

'We talked about the poem, remember?' said Laurie. 'About being a kid, about being *happiest*, and how we only think we're happy cos we party and drink and stuff. And how that's not really being happy, it's just pretending to be a grown-up.'

'Nell forgot to put her feet to the stars,' said Imogen. 'Or maybe she doesn't know how.'

And so Paul signed his name, added it to the names of his students, who didn't always have the language but who certainly understood.

'We're giving it to her tomorrow,' said Imogen. 'Me and Helena.'

He didn't say, *Helena and I.*

'And Nell thinks the other girls can start visiting her now.'

He told them that their friendship would mean a great deal to her. That it might even help more than all the doctors could. And then, because he couldn't help himself, because he'd been lecturing students for years, would be lecturing until the day he died, he told them about Carl Jung.

'He was a famous psychoanalyst,' he said. 'He spoke to many troubled, unhappy people, gave them the benefit of his complex theories and many years of training. But in the end he believed he did nothing that a good friend couldn't have done. Listen. And show they care.'

Helena gave him a puzzled look. 'So *that's* how you pronounce it,' she said. 'Jung. I thought it rhymed with *dung.*' She beamed at her classmates. 'I'm reading his work on the collective unconscious. It's very deep.'

They began to straggle out but Helena stood at the door, looking up at him.

'Mr H,' she said, and paused. 'Do you really think Nell will get better?'

Paul breathed in deeply, folded his arms. Helena frowned.

'You always fold your arms,' she said, 'when you don't know what to say.'

He nodded. 'Well, you know I can't answer that question, Helena,' he said. 'No one can. Nell has...well...it's a very serious illness. But she's trying hard. And wanting to see you and the other girls, it sounds like she's turning a corner.'

'She wants to make a connection, you mean?'

'Yes. Exactly.'

Helena's eyes lit up. '*Only connect*,' she said. 'That was the epitaph in this novel I read last week.'

He didn't say *epigraph*.

'Only, here's the thing,' she went on, excited. 'This guy in the story, he wants to connect with other people and improve his life and you feel really sorry for him, but he gets killed in the end – by a bookcase falling on top of him, of all things. I mean, I like reading and all, I love it, but what a way dumb way to die.' She grinned. 'When I die,' she said, 'I'd rather have my feet to the stars.'

'I was thinking the same thing,' said Paul. 'So maybe I should start practising my handstands.'

'Metaphorically speaking.'

'Metaphorically speaking.' He looked at her closely. 'Are you happy, Helena?' he said.

She considered his question for some time, as though it were a large, unfamiliar object she had to slowly walk around, try to take in.

'I have friends who make me happy,' she said. 'And reading. And my collection of Elvis Costello records.' She looked up at him, her scarred and pitted face flushed with pleasure.

Not much of a looker, her father had pronounced.

He waved her to the door. 'Shall we walk down the stairs?' he said.

'Just watch your step,' said Helena. 'My dad fell down here last week and broke his ankle, so now he can't play golf and he's really mad.' She smiled at him. 'That made me happy, too,' she said. 'I mean, I know that's an awful thing to say, but—I'm being *authentic*. You gave us that word, remember?'

He smiled in return, and they walked down the stairs in silence. He saw her head held high, shoulders pulled back, and he felt his own feet beneath him, as light as a young man's. She would find her way, he thought, this curious, engaging child who loved to read and who knew that her father was a waste of space. And maybe he would find his way, too, at the dinner. It was a small enough thought, a big enough thought, for both of them, walking down a set of stairs; for Nell in her solitary room; and perhaps for the woman who was kind and smart and played the flute like an angel. All of them waiting, suspended, hoping to be ready for whatever might come next.

The Inner Life

Those pills the guy at the hostel gave me for the plane, they haven't knocked me out like he said they would. They haven't even stopped me thinking. Is Charlie angry with me? Or maybe she's worried or scared, but how would I bloody know when she won't answer my calls or texts? I squirm in my seat; should get up and have a stretch, do push-ups or something, but the guy next to me is spread across the armrest and blocking my way and if he starts with his snoring again I'll…Forty, fifty years old, he must be, in a T-shirt with 'The New Pornographers' plastered all over it, thinking he's so cool. I put on my headphones and check the screen for movies but it's just a bunch of stupid rom-coms and mindless action stuff. Why do people think blowing other people up is entertaining? I take off the headphones, slump back in my seat. Four hours still to go, and all I want is to see her, talk to her. *She lost a baby, Joe.* Outside the National Gallery in freezing cold London with all the pigeons flying around and Zoe phoned me: *just calling to say hi*, she says, and *it's so friggin' hot here hottest summer on record* and *how cool to have snow* and then it all came rushing out. About the baby. And when I found my voice I said, *is Charlie alright? Why didn't she tell me? Why?* And Zoe said, *she's OK, Joe, everything's OK.*

Such a dumb word. *OK.*

So first no one tells me anything and then Zoe tells me bits and pieces and I don't know what to do with these fragments she's given me. Tramping round the place, checking out the world. I was gunna look at all the famous paintings, my last big chance, but instead I went back to the hostel. Curled up like a kid and wished I could fall sleep.

The sky through my window's so blue and not a cloud anywhere, so bright I have to turn away. Trying not to look at the guy in his stupid T-shirt, his head thrown back against the seat. He's out for the count now and that's not fair, either.

The New Pornographers. They're a crap band, anyway.

You know you're back in Perth when there are no warnings every twenty seconds about unattended luggage and a beagle's wagging its tail and the guy at customs says, *g'day*, waves you to the door like he'll meet you later at the pub. Then I walk out, looking, and Mum's there, flapping her hands like some girl at a rock concert when she sees me. I feel my heart drop inside me but I fold her up and give her the biggest hug because I *am* pleased to see her, really pleased. Feeling her arms around me, helping me to breathe. She rubs my stubbly face and *dear Joe*, she says. I hitch up my rucksack, tell her I want to get going. Go home.

I try not to walk too fast, I've forgotten how short her legs are and she's telling me I look thinner and did I eat properly? Outside now and the heat hits me in the face, almost knocks me out. Forgotten this as well. *Hottest summer on record*, she says, and I tell her I already know, kind of snap at her, standing in front of the parking machine and she looks at me all pained and tells me she's sorry and I tell her I'm just really tired. And I'm sorry, too.

The air con in the car still isn't fixed: she's decided not to, *fuel efficiency, pollution and all that*, she says, and she winds down the window. Like she's trying hard. I look out and see the same old massive fake cactus in front of the fake Spanish motel, the gross pizza and hamburger joints and some new and incredibly ugly vomit-brown apartments with no windows. And all the thundering trucks so Mum has to shout now and I can't hear what she's saying as another one roars past. Road works everywhere, a four-lane highway turning into eight, or is it six? The only thing that saves this city is water: the pure, clean ocean, and a river winding through a dead heart of steel and glass and money. I can't wait to get out of this joint.

'So it was good, Joe?' she's saying. 'You'll have to tell me all about it. And photos? We can have a photo night.'

I nod, lean my head against the window.

I jolt upright and look around. We're sitting in the car and we're in our driveway.

'You nodded off,' Mum says. 'We're home.' She's smiling full on. 'I was just wondering,' she says. 'Looking at you while you were asleep…wondering where all the years have gone.'

Gone gangbusters, I think. Nineteen going on twenty, intrepid bloody traveller, globe-trotting Joe. Who made

Charlie pregnant and then she lost it and I don't even know what to feel.

'I could sure use a shower,' I say.

So I phoned her and told her I was back and all she said was *it's better not to see each other.* And so I started kind of yelling at her; I don't know what the fuck got into me, and she hung up. Sent me a text straight away: *dont call me again ever.* I mean, how can she say that? I don't know how it happened or what happened but it must've been pretty awful and sad. I said I'd use a condom but she said, no, it was fine, she was on the pill, and I believed her, why wouldn't I? And it's not like I'm in control here; it's not like I've had sex with millions of girls. Only one to be exact, before Charlie, and it wasn't all that great, we were both kind of drunk, and I remember thinking next day, OK, it's done now, no big deal. But Charlie, she was different. Danced like a crazy thing but really smart and warm. She made me feel good just holding her, not being in a hurry. And talking. And when I told her I was going travelling for a couple of months, that was all OK, too. We said we'd stay in touch and we did, and I even sent a postcard of the Catacombs in Paris, hoping she'd think that was neat.

She lost a baby. That's the only thing I know for sure.

It's really windy at the beach today so there's no one here except surfers on those big booming waves, sleek in their black wetsuits. I could never do that, out so far, just me and those waves; you'd have to be kind of crazy. Man against the elements, hey? I'm not that brave.

I can't stop thinking about her. How she told me what she wanted and how she asked me what I wanted and that felt good, too, really good, it was exciting just telling her. The words. But she cared as well. I mean, it didn't feel all mechanical, it was like it mattered, just lying together and taking our time. It was her and it was me. Charlie. Joe. And then what would've happened if she hadn't lost the baby? One of Zoe's friends had an abortion and it just broke her up, she was never the same again. Would Charlie have done that? At least let me know? All that time, when I'm sitting on trains and going to all those galleries and cathedrals and pubs, maybe she was scared out of her mind. She should've called me and I would've come home.

I could've been a father. And that seems so unreal. I mean, what do you wanna be when you grow up, Joe? A doctor or a vet? Drive a fucking fire truck? I just wanna talk to her, that's all.

The sand's whipping my face now, that stinging feeling I remember. It's the feeling of my childhood, and my dad wrapping me up in a great big towel. I see him every other year when he flies down from Queensland, and a few times I've been there myself. Waterworld and Dreamworld and all that stuff you like when you're a kid. He got married again to a nurse, like Mum, but that didn't last long, either. Mum told me once about her own marriage to Dad. She said there was no one to blame, it was just a bad mistake.

'Meet me at the cafe,' I said to Zoe. 'Just meet me.'

'She's not really talking to me either,' she says. 'Just a few texts and she says she's OK but that's all I know.'

Zoe clasps my hands and hers are as warm as toast and it settles me. We've grown up together. We know each other like no one else.

'You feel gutted, don't you?' she says. She lets her hands rest in mine and then takes them away and I want them back.

Our coffee arrives and we both sit back and Zoe points out the leaf on top, *so delicate*, she says. And have I seen the guy who does 3D animals in the froth? Kittens and crocodiles – you can watch it on YouTube. And how she's going to TAFE to study fashion design and how fashion's really art. She tells me there's this cool guy who makes dresses shaped like a teardrop, so beautiful it made her cry. She's got these amazing violet-coloured eyes, Zoe has, and all the guys fall for her but we've never felt like that about each other. Then I tell her how I might not go back to uni. She stops drinking her coffee and says, 'You're not going all downhill are you? Over Charlie? You're clever, Joe, don't waste your brains working in that bottle shop.'

'That bottle shop paid for my trip,' I say, and then I hear what else she's telling me. 'And *you're* clever, too,' I say. 'You don't have to go to uni.'

'Yeah, that's what Mum reckons. Only she says it so much it drives me nuts.'

So then I tell her it's not only Charlie and it's hard just saying her name. It's kind of other stuff as well, how I didn't do that great at uni and how philosophy's fun and challenging and all but it's not gunna do much in the world. Except maybe help people think rationally, you know, like that's ever gunna happen in this place, is it? And then I tell her about Florence, how I went inside a cathedral, not one of the famous ones but there was gold everywhere and huge chandeliers and this priest in a deep purple robe with these really heavy folds. And then I go outside and right there on the doorstep, there's this beggar with his bowl and he's all bent over and his hands are gnarled and his face looks like he's dead inside.

'So what do I do, talk Socrates with him? A bunch of Jean-Paul Sartre?'

'So what did you do?'

'Gave him some money. Which doesn't help, either.'

Zoe puts her hand on mine again. 'Just give it some time,' she says. 'You don't have to solve the world's problems when you're nineteen years old.'

'You're sounding very philosophical,' I say, and she gives me the finger.

I'm feeling better, sitting in the sun with Zoe, and the coffee's as good as she said it would be. The place belongs to one of her friends so she's trying to support it, and they don't sell baby-fucking-cinos. The sun's shining on Zoe's hair now: it's gold and kind of fluffy and there are trees full of leaves behind her; she's a painting in a frame. Maybe it would be easier if I liked her – sexually, I mean – but I just don't go for her in that way. You either do or you don't, I guess.

'You could go round and see her,' she says. 'What's the worst that could happen?'

I try to picture it.

'She could slam the door in my face. Scream at me.'

'And would that be any worse than now?'

I don't phone to let Charlie know I'm coming. She might not be home or someone else might be there, but I'm already seeing myself with my foot inside the door saying I won't leave until she explains. I never thought of going round and now I'm thinking maybe I didn't really want to see her after all, deep down, but I'm still walking.

It's not too hot today, a bit of a let off after days and days of steaming heat. It's like the summers go on forever, start in October and end in September. I check my phone, nine o'clock, and then I remember: she's got lectures at eight in the morning. *How can you do that?* I asked her, and she told me it was easy. Because she loves maths. I don't get it, never got it at school, but she told me how maths is beautiful: it has purity; it's almost cold, like a statue. And I'm lying in her arms, we've just had sex at her friend's place and I remember it, can't stop remembering how kind of wild she was and so loud at the end and it excited me again, and then she starts talking about maths and statues and she's blowing my mind, she's so damned smart. She's the first person in her family to go to uni and they think she's kind of weird and her dad keeps saying, *all you need to do is add up and stuff, what's the big deal?*

Are you the first person, too, Joe? she asked me, and I told her how my mum has a nursing degree. *Not your dad, then*, she said, and so I told her that stuff, too, but how I don't really miss him because you can't miss something that you don't really know. She didn't say anything cos she knew there was nothing to say and she put her arms around me, with her white spiky hair all damp with sweat and she doesn't wear any stuff on her face, she's just pure. But not cold. She wasn't cold, ever.

She might be sitting in a lecture room right now, paying attention. Not giving a shit about me.

I nearly get run over by these crazy cyclists with their arses way up in the air, and joggers, too they're everywhere. And people with dogs, people on bikes just for fun. A mum with a pusher and a little kid jumping up and down next to her, bursting with life. Sunny Perth. Fresh air, people running, pedalling, jumping. All the beaches. That guy in my English tute, he said he blamed the sun, how there's too much of it in *Or-stralia, hence people cultivate the life of the body instead of the inner life.* What a wanker, I mean who says *hence* when they're at home?

I check my phone again and it's ten minutes since the last time and the sun's getting hot on my back. More people on bikes, as swift as birds, darting and weaving. Maybe I should get on a bike, ride around Australia. Ride around the world. There was some guy on TV, some writer, who said he just walked all the time, all day, every day, for miles and miles. He said that walking was a way of finding yourself, who you really were, unplugged from a GPS, an iPod. That walking was a fight against corporate control. So maybe riding a bike would be kind of the same. You'd be using technology, sure, but you wouldn't have to be plugged in, it'd be just you and the road and the great outdoors. Maybe Karl would be into that, I could ask him. Haven't caught up with him since I got back.

Self, that was the guy's name. *Will Self.* Which is a cool kind of name for a writer.

So I'm outside Charlie's house now and all I can do is stop and stare, it's so ugly. That yellow brick that looks like limestone but isn't, and that bloody fake lawn. Don't they know about the toxins? From recycled rubber? But I'm walking up the path to the front door and my heart's beating fast now and I pull myself up straight. Knock four times. Trying not to be too loud. I wait. Hear footsteps inside and the door opens and it's Charlie peeping out and she's as beautiful as ever, with that spiky white hair and the biggest smoky grey eyes. We don't say a word, just stand there staring at each other and then she opens the door and steps aside to let me come in. My heart's still racing and I'm taking deep breaths and my hands are bunched up tight. She looks…she looks like nothing's different.

'I said not to,' she says.

'Well, I'm here now.'

I want to take her in my arms and just hold her but I know that'll make it worse. Then she nods to follow her. Into her room. She closes the door and there's nowhere to sit except on her bed. She sits down and I sit down next to her, not too close, and everything feels weird, it feels like we're in a play or something. But I make a start, I want to make a start.

'I wanted to see how you were…are,' I say.

'I'm fine.' She's looking at me dead straight and her face is almost angry. 'OK?' she says. 'End of story.'

I don't know what to do with this tangled-up stuff. Her hostility. But I tell her I feel bad. For what happened to her. And how I don't understand, how she said she was on the pill. And I can hear it in my voice, accusing her, and *are you saying I'm a liar*, she says. Well, she was definitely taking it, for six whole months, and she's getting really mad and I think she might scream at me. But then she stops. She looks at me all hard and kind of steely.

'I got really sick for a few days and I was throwing up all over the place. And so the pill didn't work, did it?'

Her eyes are grey as winter.

'I would have come home if you'd told me,' I say.

'That's why I didn't.'

I'm just not getting it. I don't get her at all.

'It was my baby, too, Charlie,' I say. 'We could have...I would have helped you if you'd wanted me to.'

'Well, I'm glad you think it was *your* baby,' she says.

Her voice is so cold now it's hurting and I've got nothing to hang onto. 'Why wouldn't I, Charlie?' I say, 'what are you talking about?'

'Haven't you heard? What people say about me?'

I don't say a word.

'Like, I'm a slut,' she says. She's looking at me real close, almost daring me to speak. But then her face kind of softens and it's a heart, her face, so tiny, so pale. 'There was only you, Joe,' she says quietly. 'When we were sleeping together. I would never have done that to you.'

It's like this great big world of other people is going on around me, without me, how I don't know a goddamn thing, and she's sitting there in front of me and I don't know her either.

'It wasn't bad,' she says calmly. Out of the blue. 'I was only seven weeks and there wasn't much blood...And I wouldn't have kept it anyway.'

She doesn't use the word.

There's a loud knock on the door, and a loud voice.

'Charlotte? If you want that lift you'd better get a move on. I'll be in the car.'

We wait for the footsteps to disappear. Charlie tells me I can go out the back if I want: her brother's at home but he's asleep in his room; he's always asleep. So I get up, turn at the door for one last look.

'I'll call you, OK?' I say.

She shrugs. 'Whatever.'

I open the door, look around for my escape.

You think you know someone, holding them in your arms and talking. And then you find you don't know them at all. And it freaks you out. Not knowing them.

I walk away in a hurry and don't look back, even though I want to. And then I remember the picture. That postcard of the Catacombs. I wish I'd never sent it.

I'm clearing the dishes from breakfast when there's a knock on the door, and then a bright kind of girly voice calling down the hallway. *It's Frieda*, says Mum, *remember her little boy?* I won't believe how much he's grown, apparently. Frieda comes in carrying him on her hip and he's naked, all plump and white, a jumpy fat little slug.

Mum holds out her arms but the kid hides his face in Frieda's chest. *So bloody hot*, she says, *hope you don't mind him in the nuddie; he's toilet trained*, and Mum's laughing and saying, *do I look that old?* And I'm watching the two of them talking and laughing and all the time the kid's hiding. Then Mum starts on about me, *here's Joe*, she says to Frieda. Talk about stating the bleeding obvious. *Just back from Europe, remember?* And then she's on about the pancakes I made for breakfast, *so yummy, you wouldn't find better in a cafe.* Here is my son: Exhibit A. And then the kid swivels round and he sees me, looks me up and down and then lets out this huge great scream, *don't let the giant get me!* And he's hiding away, then looking again, hiding again. Mum brushes back his hair, all gold and curly and damp with sweat, and tells him I'm a very friendly giant who looks after little boys.

Joe the friendly giant. Someone should write a book.

Now Mum's scrambling in a cupboard and next thing you know he's a drummer, this naked little kid sitting on the floor and banging a saucepan with a wooden spoon. *Your favourite toy as a child, Joe,* says Mum. Telling you things you can't remember, it's like your identity doesn't belong to you. She bends down in front of the kid and he gives her an almighty whack on the face with his spoon. Mum's laughing but Frieda's upset, tells the kid to say sorry. Liam. That's his name. *Sorry,* he says, in this tiny little voice and I walk to the sink and turn my back cos I'm trying not to cry.

She said it like it didn't even matter. Charlie.

Yesterday down at the beach I nearly said something to Karl. He thought I looked a bit down but I didn't want to say. He's a really strong swimmer, pounds through the waves, and he does weights and all, so I tell him about my idea. Cycling round Australia. He said sure, why not, maybe next summer. He's not a great talker, Karl. He saves up his words for when they matter. Like when we were at this party and this guy he was seeing got stuck into him, called him all sorts of names and said some pretty private stuff in front of everyone, everyone staring. But Karl just stood up straight and said, *thanks for being a really good friend, the kind that stabs you in the front.* I told him later that was cool.

I've been up since six o'clock, an early morning swim. Part of my new self-improvement plan. There's only a few surfers and a bunch of old guys who swim every morning, all through the year, doesn't matter how cold it is. They belong to some old guys' club. I saw it in the local paper, how they've been coming here for thirty years or something. I reckon that's neat, to know people all that time and maybe being old wouldn't be so bad. Maybe you've left a lot of shit behind you. Like, just get in that water and enjoy every moment. Just feel glad to be alive.

And then my mobile rings and it's Karl, and he's telling me he didn't make that up, you know, the line about a good friend stabbing you in the front. Someone else said it first, he says, it was Oscar Wilde, but he was trying to impress everyone and he just wanted me to know. And I think that's kind of nice, telling me. It's ethical. So I tell him that's OK, it doesn't matter anyway, because someone else always says things first.

That discussion in my philosophy tute. *Originality, authenticity, sincerity,* trying to understand the difference. It really did my head in.

I should have gone to the Greens meeting but they emailed another bloody massive agenda. Last time I went, before Europe, before a whole lot of other stuff, it took forever just to get through Apologies. Then I hear this knock on the door. Mum's at work so I know I have to answer and I'm thinking it's one of those God-botherers, the ones who bring their kids along. I really hate that, the little boys in ties for Christ's sake, or the little girls in frilly white dresses. I mean, what fucking chance do they have? And there's knocking again and OK, OK, I'm going down the hallway, ready to tell them I don't need to be saved or maybe I can use Karl's line, that I'm a Satanist with cannibalistic tendencies. I open the door and it's her: Charlie. I stop myself from saying what are you doing here cos she's got that look on her face again. Steely.

'So, are you gunna ask me in?' she says.

She's in jeans and a black T-shirt and her arms are so bare and golden brown and she knocks me out again. So I stand aside and let her pass, watch her watching me.

'You said you'd call me,' she says. All defiant.

'And you said, *whatever.*'

Her face kind of puzzles up.

'I didn't know what else to say.'

And so I take her in my arms and hold her against me, my face against hers. All I know is I've never felt like this before, this girl in my arms who just *fits.*

'We messed up, didn't we?' she says.

I take her hand, lead her into my room and we sit on my bed. Just sit.

'I was scared,' she says, and she's looking at me closely now. 'I was scared you'd think I tricked you. I should have trusted you.' She takes my hand, just holds it softly. 'I take the pill because I know I want to have sex,' she says. 'That's not being a slut, that's just being sensible.'

I tell her she doesn't have to defend herself to me and she tells me she isn't, that she just wants me to know who she is. And I can see it now, real clearly: that I'm only just getting started.

'So *was* it bad?' I say, and she shakes her head.

'It happened so quick and there wasn't any pain, really.' She's still holding my hand. 'I didn't want to keep it,' she says. 'The baby.'

'And I wouldn't...it would have been your choice,' I say.

I put my hand over hers. We fit.

'It did make me feel sad,' she says, 'but most of all it made me angry, my body stuffing up like that.' She looks at me closely again, with those dark grey eyes that undo me. 'But just so you know,' she says, 'I don't want you to be full of pity and *hey, Charlie, how awful* and all that. I don't want what happened to...define us.'

'Us,' I say.

She puts her hand on the back of my neck, pulls me towards her. Kisses me softly, so softly, and we fall back on the bed and lie together in each other's arms and keep very still. And it's good, the stillness. The waiting. When I know there's so much to wait for.

So Mum wants to know what I'm doing, packing stuff into the esky at this hour of the morning. I tell her I'm going on a picnic. *With Karl?* she says, tilting her head to the side like she always does when she wants to ask but kind of knows she shouldn't. I tell her it's no one she knows, it's someone called Charlie, and I feel my face going red.

'Her real name's Charlotte,' I say, and I'm feeling even redder. So I say how it's not her real name but her legal name and there's a philosophical difference. Mum's smiling away now and would Charlie like to come to dinner sometime, she says. She's got that look in her eyes like I know she's happy for me, how she's always saying she just wants me to be happy, and so before I know it these words come stumbling out.

'Do you ever miss him?' I say.

'Who?'

'My dad.'

She looks startled.

'Never,' she says. 'Why are you asking me?'

And I want to say, *it's your inner life, tell me about your inner life*, but I think she might just laugh and tell me all about her kidneys and intestines and all the nurse stuff. So I shrug and say it's just that I've never asked her before. Her face goes all soft and she walks over to me and wraps her arms around me, gives me a gentle hug but doesn't let me go. And I rest for a moment in her warmth, feeling safe, the way I've always felt with Mum.

So maybe I will ask Charlie to dinner even though I'm not too sure she's the kind of girl you ask to meet your mum.

But then again, maybe she's not any kind of girl. Maybe she's Charlie.

Your Body is a Temple

'You are not going to believe what I did today!'

It's ten o'clock and I'm ready for bed but Bea knows she can phone me anytime.

'I just bought the florist's!'

I'm speechless but it doesn't matter because Bea's gushing out all her news like she always does. *All those years of hard work, Annie,* she says, *you know I've done the lot,* and I do, I've heard it many times: the five am run to the flower markets, the hauling heavy buckets, changing slimy water, all *the unglamorous stuff* that people don't know about. *It's not all scones and jam,* she likes to say, as though she works in a cake shop. And then her voice goes quiet. Has she done the right thing? All that money. What'll happen, she says, when she's old and sick or dying and her Rachael isn't there?

'I mean, your friends are your friends, but it's family who stick by you in the end.'

I tell her she's a long way from the end and that whenever it comes I'll take care of her, just as she'd do for me. And she's happy again, with all these plans for a new paint job, a new computer system, music in the background, fancy wrapping paper and cards; she wants cards with beautiful words, not the Hallmark crap, and she hasn't been this happy since— she can't remember. When she first held Rachael in her arms.

'I used the money from my ex,' she says. She always calls him that; or *the bastard* when she's had a few too many; *fucking prick* when she's more or less under the table. I've almost forgotten his name.

'And, hey, there's this other thing…'

This time I know where she's heading. A new man, another *funny* one, weird in a harmless kind of way. Brad, I think he's called, or is it Bob? Some guy she picked up in her yoga class, *cos he sure couldn't pick me up*. She's been telling that joke for years.

'And so, Annie,' she says, 'we finally make it into bed and he asks me to keep my shoes on. So I'm thinking, *here we go again*, and the bloody foreplay went on for so long I was starting to lose interest. But then he lifts his arms up to the ceiling and says, in this guru kind of voice: *your body is a temple*. And I say, *Well, then, just take my bloody shoes off and come inside.*'

'You didn't!'

'I don't think he got it but it didn't matter anyway because…it's well and truly over.'

She gives me another story. How she caught a glimpse of her ex last night and he was literally holding the baby and looking pretty pissed off and his child bride was looking like Posh, all bones and scowling. Like her mum's just nicked her cigarettes.

'How did she ever give birth?' she says. 'If she turned side on, you'd call the Missing Person's Bureau.'

You have to laugh: her motto. You have to.

I remember Bea's ex turned up in the driveway with a red Volkswagon Golf for Rachael's birthday and next day Rachael hired a chainsaw, gouged the car all over and drove it back to his place. She'd forgotten money for a bus fare but didn't mind walking, singing in fact, ten kilometres to get home.

I can't wait to see what Bea's done to the shop. Only I have to remember to call it a florist's. She can get a bit sniffy about that because *it's not just about money*, she says, it's about bringing together her two favourite things: people and flowers. And I must say, she's very good at arranging both of them. I've seen her in action, turning the crabbiest customer into a beacon of smiles, or adding a few trimmings to a bouquet when the person doesn't have much money. I've even seen her patch up a couple of dodgy relationships. All the stories she tells me: the German migrant whose wife of fifty years didn't recognise him anymore; the teenage boy who'd made his mother cry; the woman who bought flowers for herself to make her boyfriend jealous; the woman who bought a bouquet every week for her daughter who had three young kids and was going quietly mad in the suburbs. And all you have to do, Bea says, is ask them if the flowers are for a special occasion.

When I walk into the shop, I see she must have asked the question, because an elderly man, eighty if he's a day, is leaning on the counter, giving Bea an earful about his new romance. A dating site on the internet for the over sixties, and suddenly he's *rejuvenated*. I know what that's a code for and I try not to picture it. And then I catch myself feeling resentful, since the last time I had sex was five years and three months ago. I look around while he's rabbiting on, and the place is what people call a riot of colour: brilliant reds, dusty pinks, deepest purples, twinkling blues, sunset oranges. I don't know the names of any of the flowers except the roses and poppies; flowers that bend or nestle or reach out to something inside you. And the smell. Bea insists on *fragrance*: sweet and dark at the same time, like a mild kind of swoon. I smile at the rejuvenated man as he walks out the door, and Bea flashes me one of her looks, wants to know if I noticed the bouquet she made him. Lilies, freesias, narcissus, she says, like a song. And did I see *the composition*?

I remember the first time she told me about her love affair with flowers. We were sixteen years old and sneaking out of school and we used to sit in coffee shops drinking long blacks and trying to look bored in a meaningful kind of way so boys would notice us. When you arrange flowers, she said, when you put them in a vase or a basket or make a bouquet, it's all about the lines and spaces, the rhythm and the harmony. I told her to say that in class, she sounded so clever; but she said she'd read it in a book and, anyway, the other kids would think she was a wanker. She tried to teach me once how to make those lines and spaces, but I was hopeless; she said I didn't have a green finger to my name. *But that's for gardening*, Bea said. *You don't need green fingers to work with flowers.* Just practice, and some patience.

Patience. I was never any good at that, either. Couldn't wait to get married, couldn't wait to get pregnant, couldn't wait to see the back of him. But that's another story.

And I remember the first time I walked into Bea's new townhouse, after her divorce. There was a mammoth vase of flowers in the living room, towering and twirling and full of light.

'Agapanthus and golden rod,' she said. 'Isn't it surprising?'

The doorbell rings and when I open the door Bea collapses into me, throws her arms around me and tells me I'm *not going to believe this*. Again. I guide her down the hallway and sit her down and she's bursting and laughing, all of her flowing in a long red caftan. She's just met this man, she says, and no, it's not what I think. He wants to make a movie; well, a documentary, and she's giggling like a girl, says she's going to be a star, a doco star, a movie star. He saw the name of the florist's and thought it sounded *lyrical*: Marigold's.

'So when he comes in,' she says, 'I was reading a book.' She's smiling away, a bit cat-got-the-cream. 'It's all about the history of flowers, the art of floriography. That's the biggest word I've used in my entire life. And so he asks me all about it and—'

She's away; unstoppable. How she told this guy all about the chapter she was reading, about *the olden days*, when people used flowers to show their feelings because you weren't allowed to speak them. And not just the colour, not just red roses for passion, the obvious stuff. It was the size of the bouquet, the shape, even the hand you held them in to

71

present them to the loved one. All of it had a special meaning, a secret code of feelings. These days, she told him, anyone could point to a bunch of roses, whip out the old credit card; but people had to be more subtle in the olden days.

'And he was really rapt, Annie, hanging on every word. And the next thing you know he's asking me to appear in his doco, to talk about Marigold's and this book and I'm just—well, nothing like this has ever happened to me before.'

'So, did he ask you for any money?'

Bea looks offended. 'Not a cent,' she says. 'He asked me out to dinner to discuss things. Next Saturday night. I mean, it's just fantastic publicity as well. And he sounded very savvy, said that people are getting tired of cooking shows and home renovation and how flowers are going to be the next big thing. That his show would explain *the artistry*. God, I'm already seeing it, Annie: the whole red carpet bit—'

'What's his name?'

'Rex.'

'Rex what?'

'Just, Rex.'

'You mean—Well, what's the name of his company?' I say. 'Did he leave you a business card? Did he—'

But she waves me away, says she'll find out everything when they meet for dinner. 'Honestly, Bea—' I say, but she cuts me off, says she's not a babe in the woods, and Rex was intelligent and sensitive and urban. 'Urbane,' I say, and she shrugs.

'So I bet he was really good-looking.'

She tosses her head slightly. 'Well, yes, in a Pierce Brosnan kind of way. And he was wearing a really well-cut suit and very shiny shoes.'

I want to know what *very shiny shoes* have to do with anything and she tells me I'm being so negative. Grouchy.

'Be happy for me, Annie,' she says. 'You're my very best friend.'

We drink champagne and Bea's all flappy, already imagining a brand new dress. There's a famous saying, isn't there: beware of anything that needs new clothes? Or was it something about emperor's clothes? Either way, I'm not saying anything. I pour us another glass.

For the next few days I get a rush of phone calls, each one more excited than the last. She says the waiting's really getting to her: she's worried she'll come out in hives. And Rachael phones me twice to tell me she's so proud of her mum. Dear girl. She'd kill for her mum, maybe with a chainsaw. Bea told me once it was the only thing she ever liked about her ex, how he'd given her this beautiful child. I'm remembering all this as I'm sitting at home alone, drinking alone, and thinking how strange it must be to have this child who's the spitting image of her father. Strong jaw and cheekbones, and those bedroom eyes. And how kind of sad it must be as well. And how relieved I am that both of mine take after me. Except for Stevie's eyes, which in a certain light are the same murky blue as his deadbeat father's.

And then the big day finally arrives. Bea comes over at eight am, pulls me out of bed and begs my opinion on the choice of two dresses. Wants me to be ruthlessly honest. Does the bright green number look too showy? A bit trashy, even? And, yes, she knows the black one's slimming, but it's a bit too...

'Predictable?' I say, as I watch her twirl around. 'Predictable is good, Bea. And it makes you look classy. Wear them with your pearls.'

And then she drags out ten shades of lipstick from her bag, lines them up in a row. And mascara. She just paid fifty-two whole dollars for mascara, can I believe that? Estee Lauder: Sumptuous *and* Extreme, apparently. So by the time we've been through the make-up, the hair, the shoes and whether a ring on each hand is one too many, I'm secretly pleased to see the back of her. My best friend. My best friend since first year high school. I remember the day I brought her home and my mother went into a fit. All that black stuff around her eyes, she said, and far too much flesh on display.

And what would I do without that flesh, that consoles me, comforts me?

I picture Bea in her classy black dress, sitting down to dinner. It's Saturday night, and there's nothing on TV and I try not to pour another glass of wine. And then the next thing I know, it's morning. How did that sunlight sneak into the room? I mope my way to the bedroom and fall right back into sleep. And then it's one in the afternoon and my mouth is like a desert. Bea used to spell it *dessert*. I grope for my mobile, expecting a message, some kind of I-told-you-so text with a thousand girly kisses. But there's nothing, not even the usual message that my mobile account's running out. So I make myself get up and have a healthy breakfast that's turned into lunch: homemade muesli with half a banana. Finish it off with half a block of Cadbury's. I'll save the rest for dinner. Or maybe I'll have dinner with

Bea. She can take me out to celebrate. I half-expect her to call but nothing's happening. Think about calling myself, but madam's probably still asleep, wined and dined and comatose, with her Sumptuous and Extreme running down her cheeks.

I do a spot of gardening in the afternoon sun. Not that *garden*'s exactly the right word for my overgrown geraniums and weedy patch of lawn in need of mowing. Jake the lawnmower guy will be here next week, or is it the week after? He used to be more focused on my breasts than on his thunderous damned machine, but he's eased off since I told him to stop staring. He said he didn't realise, it was just what men did...*Some* men, I said, *and now there's no excuse*. Still, he tells a good joke, and he must be sixty-five if he's a day.

I stop weeding, check my phone again. Nothing. Three o'clock, and still nothing. I take a shower, check my phone again. Nothing. I think about driving to see her, and then think I'll just leave her alone. Drive to the bottle shop instead. It's much further than the supermarket but the specials are always good, and the guy behind the counter is very...sweet. A soft kind of face and a soft way of talking. I love the way he always says: *and will that be all for today?* I mean, of course it's not all. I'd rip his shirt off if I thought I was in with a chance. And as I'm driving, my phone starts ringing. And ringing. I know I have to pull over because cops in unmarked cars are checking people out. *Fucking cops*, my ex used to say. A lot. It could have had something to do with his breaking-and-entering and what's known in politer circles as domestic violence. I get to the phone before it stops and it's Bea, pleading to see me in a hurry. She's all twitchy and breathless, will explain everything when she sees me but *don't worry, Annie, I'm still alive.* Well, how can I not worry after something like that? And, yes, I'll take it slowly, I tell her, which means the usual Mr Macho Man starts revving it up behind me, trying to edge me over the speed limit. If I had my way I'd have buses on the side of the road doing RTCs. Random Testosterone Checks. I'm so flustered by all the speeding and guys giving me the finger that by the time I make it home I'm a bit of a wreck. I see Bea's car in the driveway. And she's standing on the porch looking hunched over, a bit crumpled up, which isn't like her at all. She's a stand-up-straight-and-shoulders-back kind of woman. She hurries to my car to meet me, throws her arms around me and doesn't let me go.

'You were right, Annie,' she says. 'About the doco guy.'

'He wanted money?'

'A whole lot worse than that.'

And standing in the driveway, the sun streaming down on us, her body's all shaky and she pulls away from me and, no, she doesn't even want to come in, have a stiff drink. Just wants to get it out, *the whole sordid story.*

'We agreed to meet at Le Petit Choux,' she says, 'and when I arrived, he was already waiting.'

She's sounding like a voice-over to a crime show but I don't say a word as she looks me in the eye.

'He's sitting at the table, the doco man, with another man, another Pierce Brosnan look-alike. Aubery. What kind of a poncy name is that? Both of them looking sharp in these sleek black suits, and so charming, you know, so looking-deep-into-my-eyes kind of thing. And would I prefer chardonnay or riesling? Or a red? Because I look like a woman who'd like a full-bodied cabernet sauvignon. Annie, everyone we know says *cab sav* and no one we know says *full-bodied*. Anyway, they're fussing over me, insisting I try the oysters and would I like the fish to follow, the grilled barramundi here is always superb, although the sirloin steak, medium-rare, is also very good. That kind of rubbish.'

She can remember every detail. Everything's burned on her mind.

'And so,' she says, 'there I am in a packed-to-the-ceiling five-star restaurant, looking around and thinking I'm seeing famous people. Isn't that Hugh Jackman over there – I could have sworn it was Wolverine. And that dark-skinned woman with a flashing smile, she looks like Oprah but Oprah was in Perth last year and what on earth would she be doing here two years in a row?'

I have no answer to this, or to anything, really.

'Anyway, I'm sipping my cab sav, taking it slowly, thinking they must have a lot of dough, Rex and his mate Aubrey, splashing it around at Le Petit Choux, and we're chatting away about Marigold's and how long have I owned it, what made me become a florist…Taking an interest, getting some raw material, they say. And the steak's the best I've ever had – still mooing a bit, you know.'

She takes a deep breath.

'So, Annie,' she says, 'get this. Rex leans across the table, puts his hands together and says they have *a proposition*. They're making a film but it's not about flowers, he says, unless I'd like to wear some in my hair. Well, you'd have to say that's sounding weird, and then the other guy, he leans in, too, says Rex told him I was beautiful and how I most certainly was. *Rubenesque*, whatever that was, but I had a feeling it wasn't good.'

They told her they made films about women. *All different kinds of women, in all their glorious variety.* And Bea says she's feeling really jumpy now and the Aubrey guy puts his hand over hers and says in this soft kind of voice, she can still hear it, so smooth, so sure of himself, how *it's about women making other women happy. It's beautiful. You look like the sort of woman who'd enjoy that.*

'It was porn,' Bea says flatly, and takes my hand. 'An orgy of women, to be exact. And they went on about how people have the wrong idea about what they're making, think it's mindless and immoral, but they're producing art, and art has nothing to with morals, he says. Art just *is*, or some bullshit like that.'

'So what did you say? Do?'

She says it felt like being a kid again, when some stranger gropes you in the movies and you're too frozen to say anything, do anything, you just sit there wishing it would all stop. And because I could never have imagined this – this cheap and nasty trick, this humiliation – I know I'm never going to say, *I told you so.* But then Bea straightens up, says she finally got her act together, smiled sweetly, nodded a lot as she finished her steak and the amazing cab sav. I can see a smile creeping over her face right now.

'All these fancy customers,' she says, 'not a spare seat in the house. And so I stand up and bang my fork against my glass, you know how they do, and it's like I'm some really classy compere or I'm reading out a script. *Ladies and gentlemen*, I say, *allow me to present these two gentlemen, here at this table. Rex and Aubrey. They film naked women having sex. Lots of women at the same time.* And everyone's putting down their glasses and knives and forks and just staring and the guys are really squirming in their seats but I'm only just getting started. *They claim they're making works of art*, I say, but *they're just really sleazy men in suits getting their rocks off. They're so pathetically empty they have to pay women to perform for them.* And the guys are looking down at the table with those wishing-the-earth-would-open-up-and-swallow-me faces, and I just can't stop, I'm having such a great time. *And they pay very handsomely*, I say, *so if any of you ladies here are interested, or have daughters, mothers, sisters, friends, who want to be made to feel like garbage, just approach these gentlemen here and I'm sure they'll be only too delighted to oblige.'*

I can see the stunned faces of her audience. The very red faces of those urbane, creepy men. I can see Bea, and she's fantastic.

'And what happened then?'

'Well, I ended by saying that if anyone wanted to purchase really beautiful flowers, just call in at my florist's. I thought *purchase* was better than *buy*. *Marigold's*, I said, *such a lyrical name, and I'll be very happy to satisfy your every floral requirement.* And everyone burst into applause. Then I left, just sailed out the door with a wave.'

I feel like applauding, myself.

She shrugs. 'So I had my movie-star moment in the end,' she says. 'But, god, those men, Annie. Disgusting.'

I ask her if she's alright and she nods. Still a bit shaken, and her Rachael's ropeable, wants to go to the police.

'But what can you do?' she says. 'They not doing anything illegal, are they? Just being revolting men.' She sets her mouth tightly. 'But you know what really hurt me most?' she says. 'How they didn't take me seriously. All these years, bringing beauty into people's lives, so they can look at a bouquet, an arrangement, and know that someone cares for them.'

Then she tries to brighten. Says maybe it won't turn out to be a complete waste of her time.

'My big plug for Marigold's,' she says. 'Maybe I'll have customers streaming through the door. Oh, and I googled *Rubenesque* this morning, some guy from the olden days who painted really big women. *Plump*, it said. *Fleshy. Voluptuous.*' She forces a smile. 'Make mine voluptuous,' she says.

Working it Out

She leaned forward in her chair, taking care not to spill her glass of gin.

'You'll never guess,' she said, 'the name of Beth's new grandchild. It's something to do with the weather.'

He didn't look up from his magazine. The subscription was running out but he wasn't all that fussed. The same old writers with their same old views on foreign aid, refugees, gay marriage, etcetera, etcetera, and more or less talking to themselves.

'Alan, did you hear me? The baby's name.'

He raised an eyebrow. 'Is it Cyclone?'

'Don't be silly.'

'Flood, then? Or Mudslide? Light Precipitation?'

She rolled her eyes. 'Well, if you must know,' she said, 'the baby's name is Raine. With an e.'

'Better than Chief Sitting Bull, I suppose.'

'Don't be ridiculous,' she snapped. 'It's a girl.' She took a tiny sip, then settled back in her chair. 'Anyway,' she said, 'she's a very sweet baby. Beth said that—'

He tried not to listen to all the details about hair and chin and whose eyes the baby had and how she looked straight into *your* eyes as if she already knew you and did he remember the first time he'd held their grandchildren in his arms because she certainly did. And had she told him about Beth's older son, given some big promotion and now he was taking Beth and Dougie on a holiday to the Bahamas or was it Bermuda…and on and on and on she went like never-ending rain on a dismal day so it hurt in your heart to look through any window.

Seven am, another hour before another working day. He watched her gobble as she talked, but tried not to look at the crumb of toast wedged in the corner of her mouth. It added indignity to the inanity of her monologue, expounding on the neighbours' new puppy, *certainly very cute but turning into a yapper* and *it's alright for you, Alan, because you're at work all day.*

God spare me, he thought, as she switched to the cost of bananas and strawberry jam and how chocolate was on special this week and she should stock up on the dark kind that was meant to be good for your heart but maybe she'd lash out and buy some of the milk kind with the jelly and popcorn pieces because a little bit of what you fancy…He used to love her *hearty appetite*, they called it, before the days of clogged arteries and late-onset diabetes. Her tucking in with gusto, the lavish portions: an overture, a prelude, to rolling around in bed. And my god she could roll – she was hungry for it, slurping and licking and moaning, and tender, too, gentle, as he buried himself in her curtain of hair, floating in a field of golden wheat, and she was warm and lovely and woozy with sex and he thought he would die with the pleasure.

Now, sitting across the breakfast table, he tried not to look at the wobbling, mottled flesh of her arm as she reached across for the milk. Not that he could talk, with his thickening waist and triple chin. He'd had to ask her to let out his trousers, and that didn't half made her happy, did it, stitching away smugly, now that he was joining the merry band of the overweight and slothful. But at least he'd started making an effort, three months now at the gym, among the muscular young men with barrel thighs and all the young women with bud-like breasts and tapered, silky legs, tormenting him. Even the older women, in their forties, fifties, spruce and fit and strutting, didn't give him a second glance. Oh, he'd seen those glances, and the bolder stares, checking each other out, working out, working it all out. This human parade; this throbbing, grunting, heave-ho affirmation of the modern, managerial self: I work out therefore I am, as he panted and trudged on the treadmill, an incline of seven on a really good day. Like bloody Sisyphus he was, over and over again.

The tyranny of appearances. Even men these days. He'd read that in another magazine, all the articles about gyms and botox and cosmetic surgery for men in search of eternal youth. Or a new woman, new job, new car, new suit, a tropical island wet dream. He remembered that ad on TV, a man on horseback thundering through the surf, looking, well, manly, he supposed. Flogging some potion for the ageing skin. *Because you're worth it*, apparently. And sex. The most potent fix of them all. It used up many calories, toned the muscles, expanded the lungs, energised, life-enhanced, brought you closer to some god, or gods.

*If I don't get some action soon, I'll go crazy…*He remembered young Brett at work, yesterday, over lunch. His wife, he said, didn't *put out* anymore. Al hadn't known which was worse: the crudeness of the confession, or his own middle-aged jab of recognition.

He passed Cornelia the margarine and then spread jam thinly on his toast. *A waste of calories*, the diet book called it, but what the hell. He bit off a piece and focused on his chewing, tried not to think about her putting out and rolling around and her arousing, drowsy murmurs. All so long ago now, like a dream. Or a modern fairytale. He should make one up for the grandkids: *Once upon a time there was a beautiful young woman with golden hair down to her waist who was adored by all the young men in the village. But she only had eyes for one young man, who had curly black hair and slim hips and promised her a big shining diamond ring if only she would marry him.*

He used to feel brightened with love when she walked into a room. Every time.

He noticed she'd stopped talking, that the relentless noise of banalities, repetitions, fillers, naggings, questions, snaps and nudges had suddenly stilled. He looked at her for a moment, properly, and caught a memory of the sweetness of her face in repose.

'What are you looking at?' she said sharply.

'Nothing,' he said. 'Not a damned thing.'

Sometimes he despised himself.

'So…they won't be here for Christmas,' she said.

After half an hour on the phone, this is what it came down to: their son and his wife and their two chirpy daughters, missing in action again. Al could see Cornelia's grim face as she wiped her hands on her apron.

'Bali again?' he said. Taking her side for a moment.

'No, a big one this time. Italy and France and Euro Disney. They promised the girls.'

'Well…' He made a move towards her, then stopped. 'We could have some people round,' he said.

'Let's invite the Stones,' she said briskly. 'They had us round the year before last.'

And then she was off to the kitchen, putting on a brave face. It was the one unchanging, admirable thing about his wife: that she had raised their son mindfully and loved him fiercely and tried hard to let him go. She'd lost two babies and then lost their son as well, the charming little boy who became the taciturn teen, and then the adult who looked down his tertiary-educated nose at his simple-minded mother. But she never complained; indeed, she actively defended him: he was *busy* or *stressed* or *trying so hard to be a good provider.*

Al thought he should call after her, offer to help, but he already knew her answer: *Everything's under control; pour yourself a drink, and one for me.*

She'd long ago taken refuge in drink, while he'd hidden in magazines and books. A magazine didn't stop her talking but the weight of a book sometimes cowed her into silence. She'd left school at sixteen, unread and pregnant, and miscarried six weeks after they wed. *Marry in haste, repent at leisure.* He'd read about a study that showed a strong correlation between brief courtships and divorce. As though divorce was necessarily a bad thing.

She called out from the kitchen: dinner would be ready in half an hour. And he'd forgotten her drink so could he kindly get a move on and then see what was on the telly.

Cornelia. The first time he met her, he thought her name was Cordelia. Shakespeare's tragic heroine, *her voice...ever soft, gentle and low.* He'd quoted Cornelia the line, hoping to impress, and then had to explain the allusion: the heroine's integrity and compassion, he'd said, the terrible injustice of her death. Cornelia-not-Cordelia had looked puzzled for a moment, and then let out a hoot of a laugh. *But we're all going to die in the end,* she'd said. It should have been a warning but he'd chosen to ignore it. Unable to stop himself, sliding his hands up her skirt, pushing her gently against the wall, thrusting into her. The moment of conception, born of misconception.

Brett threw down his pen and muttered, *bloody Suduko,* leaned forward in his chair. Closer; conspiratorial. With that lean and desperate look that Al was learning to recognise. And he was at it again, the sex-starved idiot, yabbering on about online porn and sending away for some toys, maybe he could spark some interest...Al had listened over several days, nodded, sighed, made the occasional sympathetic grunt, but now he was fed up, he was utterly spent. He wanted no more of these riotous excursions into the feverish human heart. Maybe he should just pack his misanthropic bag and leave town, buy a small block of land in the country and breathe in the clean, fresh air. Grow massive pumpkins and milk a cow. Become a hermit in galoshes, chase intruders off his land.

He stood up swiftly, brushed some crumbs from his trousers and went back to his desk. Faced the computer, swivelled round in his chair, faced the computer again. Work: it was meant to give your life meaning, or make you free. No, the *work makes you free* bit was Hitler. Or was it Freud? Work and love, that was it; that's what the cigar-smoking misery guts Viennese doctor had prescribed: work and love, the cornerstones of humanity. *Cornerstone*, Al said in his head. More like tombstone. He'd already chosen his epitaph, the message last week on the ATM: *Amount requested exceeds amount available*. He'd laughed so loudly that, when he turned around, people in the queue had edged away from him, given him a really wide berth.

For the sake of their guests, he tried not to be all *bah-humbug*, even though Christmas, quite frankly, gave him the shits. Every year, the same bloody stupid paper crowns, ludicrous foreign reindeers and costly spray-on snow. He'd never been a believer and the secular version was a sham: two days of gluttony, massive credit card debt, and then the post-Christmas sales, hordes of shoppers frantically returning useless goods, eager to replace them with more useless goods. Cornelia went to church though, belting out uplifting hymns with Sandra Mason. Sandy, whom Al had cornered next to the fridge many jolly Christmases ago and pressed against, groping like the drunken fool he was, and she'd fled like the mouse she was and maybe she'd confessed, whispered to Cornelia, or maybe she'd shrieked out his shame. But no one had said a thing; there were no recriminations or sulky accusations, no biff on the nose from an enraged Mr Mason.

He hadn't even fancied her, really. Sandy. She just happened to be there, standing by a fridge.

'The turkey is ever so succulent,' said Melanie, beaming round the table.

Melanie Stone and her *ever so: the grandchildren are ever so happy at their new school...the new curtains are ever so elegant.* To think he'd once fancied her, *really* fancied, lie-awake-in-bed-at-night-and-masturbate fancy...Her hair used to be as dark as night, messy and wild, curling past her shoulders. These days her eyes were bloodshot and she wore all this paste on her face. Ghoulish.

'So, Al, how's the gym going these days?' Jeff's voice from across the table.

'All good, yeah...I'm even beginning to enjoy it.' Al raised his glass. Jeff was fit and he *worked on his tan* and everyone knew he'd spent a lifetime cheating on Melanie, who must have known as well but somehow they must have worked it out. The things we choose not to see, not to speak, not to suffer.

'Alan's trying to get his blood pressure down,' said Cornelia. 'He wants to come off the pills.'

'It'll save over three hundred dollars a year.' Al couldn't believe he'd just said that.

'Did you know—' Cornelia began. A quick sip of wine and she was on her way again. She'd already done to death the email from Europe and the photo of the girls in the snow and now she was carrying on about how she'd wanted to go to Europe last year but what with her bad back and all, and how she wished she could stop taking her pills, too, the ones for her back and the other ones for her nerves. Anxiety, she said, and she'd felt so ashamed until the doctor told her that *so many people have it, Cornelia; it's the way of the world.* So nice then to go to church last night, so serene, and yes she only went at Christmas but such a good reminder wasn't it about the true meaning and Sandra such a trooper since her husband died and did they remember Sandra...The eyes of the Stones looked glazed. *The Eyes of the Stones*, he thought. It sounded like a bad rock band. And now back to the girls and did they know young Janet had won a competition where they had to write about...

Al rammed another piece of the ever so succulent turkey into his mouth. And a very thick slice of honeyed ham, with potatoes, sweet potatoes and carrots, all of it lashed with butter. Knowing he'd regret it in the morning. It used to be booze he'd regretted in the morning, until he finally gave it away. Tried to find solace in reading again. What had that writer said? *We read to know that we are not alone.* Which was true, but only up to a point, because you couldn't wrap your arms around a book. And once, just once, it was a woman he regretted in the morning. Rita, lovely Rita, like the song. They'd met at work when she came to give a talk about Occupational Health and Safety, of all things, and they'd locked eyes and somehow she'd ended up giving him her number and they'd ended up meeting in a hotel room when the family was away. Out of town, seemingly out of his mind. But when it came down to it, after all that he'd longed for, fantasised, he'd felt so guilty that he couldn't get it up. They'd stayed the night anyway, and he'd huddled with his shame while she slept very deeply, and in the morning she smiled at him crisply and they'd done it, in a manner of speaking. She hadn't suggested another meeting, and he'd fled before she'd even finished dressing.

She had long golden hair. He must have been going on forty and she told him he was beautiful.

Lovely Rita, meter maid...when it gets dark I tow your heart away.

'Alan, for the third time, pass Mel the chocolates.'

He could see the Stones giving each other *a look*. As though they were blameless. As though they were perfect. The chocolates were nestled in one of Cornelia's gold-rimmed bowls, one of a pair. He'd broken the other one last Christmas and she'd stamped her foot and said, *why are you always so clumsy?*

Always so clumsy. Maybe that belonged on his tombstone, instead.

Cornelia was *beside herself*. The family was coming back at last, just in time for the younger one's birthday. Their chisel-faced son and his pretty, snippy wife with their golden-haired girls, Janet and Lulu. What kind of a name was Lulu? Bloody tragic, that's what. Cornelia couldn't wait to see them, hear all the news...But as soon as the bloody Brady Bunch trooped through the door, there were glum faces, a burst of whining from the happy couple...how if they'd seen one more cathedral they would have screamed... trudging through gale-force winds to find museums, art galleries, closed for the season...the tourists can go to hell...

well, you could have checked online, first, Neil...well, *you've* got fingers, too, Laura...

Three weeks in Europe, Al thought, these privileged, pampered fools, when the only time he'd been abroad, he'd nearly frozen to death camping in the Bois de Boulogne, where he'd had to use those disgusting holes in the ground to take a shit.

And now Cornelia was riding to the rescue, fussing about the children, cooing over Laura's new dress, telling Neil his beard really suited him. Since when did his son have a beard? And since when had his eyes looked so old? Gifts were handed out, tea towels for Cornelia, a tie for Al proclaiming he'd been to the Sorbonne. And Cornelia rushing in with all kinds of questions about hotels and food and the cold, it must have been *unbearable*. And then: a moment's silence at last. Until little Janet piped up in her pink little voice:

'We flew in the teacups, Nanna. And then we sat up really high in these elephants with great big ears—'

'Dumbos,' said her little sister. 'There were heaps of Dumbos.'

Their mother laughed. 'They absolutely loved Euro Disney,' she said.

'And not before bloody time,' said Neil. 'All the moaning and groaning they did until we got there. I told them I'd paid a fortune for the trip and they were bloody well going to have fun whether they liked it or not.'

His sour, carping son: all his own proud work.

Cornelia passed a plate of left-over Christmas cake and blathered on about holidays and stress and needing a holiday after a holiday, isn't that right, Alan, she said, remember when we—She stopped short, looking into little Janet's eyes, which Al could see were brimming with tears, and blue like her grandmother's, cornflower blue. The little girl in her frilly dress and ribbons and something sparkly in her hair, who lifted her arms to Cornelia, climbed up onto her lap.

'I'm sleepy,' she said. Her face was pale and her eyes flickered and then they closed like a figure in a fairytale, as if she could sleep for a hundred years.

It was after six when they finally left, and the place was oddly quiet. Al waited for his wife to speak but she was staring at the door, the space where the family had been. Family. Al wanted to laugh out loud, maniacally; instead, he waited for Cornelia to get started with her sighs and laments and enduring disappointments. She stayed silent, arms folded over her chest, looking at the door. He waited for her to move, to begin clearing up, set the machine in motion. But she didn't speak, didn't move, and it began to unsettle him, with the Christmas cake sweating on a plate, his son's hard voice still ringing in his ears.

'It was like a bloody Pinter play,' he said, and sighed for some kind of effect.

Cornelia turned to him at last and her face was icy.

'It's not a play,' she said. 'It's real.'

He wanted to swat at this statement of the *bleeding obvious*, say something mildly acerbic, but the cut of her eyes stopped him dead.

'Laura's going to leave him,' she said. He heard a note of triumph in her voice. 'He's been...he's been with other women and the girls are starting to notice things and she's finally had enough.' She flicked back her head, ever so slightly, in defiance. 'Sometimes I don't love our son,' she said. 'Sometimes I don't even like him.'

Al felt a tightening in his throat. He reached out a hand but his wife stiffened, pulled back her shoulders.

'The holiday was meant to work things out,' she said. Her eyes were haughty now, imperious. 'Laura asked my advice,' she said, 'but instead I asked her...I asked her if he still held her. If he held her like his heart would stop if he lost her.'

Al cleared his throat. 'And if his eyes still brightened,' he said, 'when she walked into a room?'

'Every time,' she said.

Because

Sometimes, when I think of my childhood, I remember all the missing mothers. The one who was shattered in a sickening crush of metal. The one who died from a ravaging illness which no one dared to name. Every year we lit a candle in the school chapel and we cried: for our friends and their mothers; for our first intimations of the cruelty of life. There were also some mothers who were physically alive but more or less dead to their daughters, because they devoted their life to charity work or played too hard at tennis or bridge or, as some of us would later learn, with other mother's husbands. There was even a mother who literally took flight, in the days before flying was common, although she returned one week later, to a communal shaking of disapproving heads and a choir of condemnation: *irresponsible, selfish, reckless, unnatural.* Words pegged with daunting precision on our suburb's moral clothesline.

But my own missing mother was different; a creature set conspicuously apart. She was one who might have been baking a pie on one day, or mending her husband's shirt with conviction, but who on the next day was simply, inexplicably, gone. Who became a wraith, a ghost, whose *spirit melted into air, into thin air.* But although my case was unique among my childhood companions, I was no more deserving of compassion; for there is no delicate set of emotional scales, no keenly calibrated instrument, that can ever measure the suffering we sometimes must endure.

I was also, in many ways, a fortunate child. I had a grandma who made me sticky cakes and always let me lick the bowl with gusto. I had an aunt who liked to kiss my forehead and squeeze my cheeks; a stern but generous uncle who always gave me sixpence for improvement in my grades; three strapping male cousins whose cartwheels and horseplay were reassuring signs of vigorous bodily presence. I had a relentlessly cheery neighbour, the childless Mrs Riley, who made me exquisite dresses with lace and pearly buttons, and who, when I was very young, walked me home from school, carrying an umbrella to protect me from the melancholy rain. And then there was Jimmy, my dearest friend. I still have the photos: two gleeful babies smearing porridge over each other's faces; toddlers with bright T-shirts and chubby smiles; the two of us, gap-toothed and grinning, posing with prizes at school. Jimmy: the only one who asked me.

Above all, I had my father, who did his very best, especially for a father of his time. I remember him reading me stories at night, performing the different voices: the ugly sisters berating poor, bedraggled Cinderella; the lovesick prince pleading with Rapunzel to let down her golden hair. I remember him tucking me in at night, kissing my cheek, letting me keep a light on until I fell asleep. I can still sense that dim yellow glow in the gathering dark, still hear my father's voice telling me there was nothing to be afraid of, even as he turned on the lamp. For my fourth birthday, he baked me an enormous cake in the shape of a mermaid, with a magnificent scaly tail made out of silver foil. I know this because I have a photo in which I am standing close to that shimmering tail, holding out a plate and greedy for a slice. As I grew older, my father packed my school lunches, and taught me how to swim and dive, ride a bike. He made a delicious hot dinner every night, except on Fridays, when we ate greasy fish and chips bought from the local shop. He came to all my concerts, applauded my thumping on a helpless piano. He guided me through the maze of numbers called homework. He patted my head and called me his *wonderful girl*. These are the small things, the powerful things, that fill a child with love.

My father was also a man of reason. One who thought it best, from the outset, to tell me the truth. I can't recall exactly when he showed me the clipping from the paper, wanting, he said, to *explain*. But I do remember that the clipping was yellow with age, slightly curled at the edges, and I remember my father reading out the details of *long dark hair, medium height and build*. But *long dark hair* and *medium* didn't really explain anything, and the clothes the woman was wearing could have belonged to anyone. They could have covered a faceless dummy in the window of a shop. I remember my father's words as he returned the clipping to a plastic folder, then looked at me intently: *So your mother isn't dead*, he said. *She is missing.*

And so we prayed, father and child, at my bedside, for her safe and speedy return. Every night, and sometimes in the mornings, he would quietly ask his God for blessed intervention. But after a while, I have no idea how long, my father and I stopped praying, and after another while, we no longer went to church. And even though I missed singing the hymns, with their burnished promise of everlasting life, I didn't miss the sly glances and clucking tongues of the parishioners, who smelled to me of mothballs and obligatory pity. And because my father was a man of reason, he told me why we no longer prayed at home or in church, no longer placed our knees on the unforgiving wooden pews: because my mother had been missing now for nine whole years, she was *unlikely to ever be found.*

Do you understand, Violet? he said, and I nodded. Although I didn't understand, not really. Because, to a child, nine years seems like an eternity, forever and ever, world without end, and I couldn't begin to imagine, ever, my world without an end. But I nodded because my father had told me the truth, and because I wanted, as I always did, to please him.

Missing; unlikely to ever be found. But despite this dismal prognosis, my father tried very hard to keep my mother alive. He showed me photographs, arranged in a pale blue album, which he told me were *in order.* I saw my mother's dimples as a baby; her various disguises in fancy dress: a pirate, a gypsy, a cowgirl with a lasso. Her billowing white bridal gown, looking like the wind might sweep her up and float her into the sky. There is only one photo in close-up: a high forehead and cheekbones; a strong, straight nose; a full, firm mouth. There is also a long-distance shot: my mother standing at the water's edge, looking out to sea, one hand shading her eyes from the sun. And, last of all, the photos of the two of us together. At least that's what my father told me, because of course I didn't know myself as the lumpy shape in a bunny rug or the toddler with fluffy hair. You have to rely on someone else, someone who was there, for proof of your existence.

In these photos my mother is always looking to the side, at something invisible, outside the frame.

My father also gave me words about my missing mother. He called her *sweet* and *kind* and *shining with life*. He told me I had her dark blue eyes. I remember how this had both frightened me and filled me with remorse, as though I had stolen those dark blue eyes and kept them for myself. Aunt Jean extolled my mother's beauty: she was, it seemed, *radiant, stunning, a gorgeous creature*; while Uncle Bill, never a man of many words, simply called my mother *clever*. My grandma, her eyes wet with tears, insisted that my mother, her daughter, was *a treasure, an angel, a saint*. I remember wanting to scoop up all those words, those precious lucky charms, and hang them on a bracelet. But even when I was very young I knew this was impossible, because you can't turn words into a tiny missing mother made out of silver or gold.

What else did my father give me? What scraps and shards, what rags of passing time, through which I might recall my mother? Were there other evidential texts of more, or less, veracity? More, or less, haunting? He gave me objects: a bronze letter opener; a box of unwritten postcards; a silver hairbrush with an embroidered backing, stitched in crimson and green. All of which I saw, and continue to see, as unexceptional. But I am fond of my mother's tiny, grey pincushion in the shape of a mouse, which holds for me the pathos of the miniature; and a marcasite brooch in the shape of a bow, fashionable during her time, and fashionable once more. But whenever I look at these objects, touch them, I cannot *feel* my mother. Perhaps a bracelet or a necklace, something she had worn against her skin, might have made a difference. Or perhaps it is merely the paradox of any object from the past, its presence confirming absence. Like a photograph of the dead: you are here; you are gone.

I was two years old when my mother went missing, and she was twenty-three. I know this because of the date on the clipping: 1961. And I know that her name was Bess. It wasn't short for Elizabeth or even Eliza: regal names, jaunty names. *Bess* felt so leaden and I wished it could have been different. Grandma urged me once to wish upon a star, but I could never see the point of that, either.

Did people ever ask me how it felt? How *I* felt? My father never did; at least, not as far as I remember. But after all this time, I cannot judge him. For, although he was an unusual father for his time – gentle, attentive, affirming – he was also a man for whom any talk of feelings must have seemed unmanly, morally flabby, even dangerous. *Feelings* might lead to that squat, grey building at the top of the hill: the asylum for the insane. Aunt Jean certainly didn't ask me how I felt. The only questions she posed, her manicured hands fluttering in the air, concerned the cutting of my hair or the blemishes on my skin. She, too, seemed to dodge and weave the world of feelings; perhaps she, too, was afraid, or perhaps she was merely shallow. Uncle Bill continued to ask about my progress at school, especially in Maths. Mrs

Riley *almost* asked me; her questions, I can see this now, were tiny hints, clues for me to confess: how did I feel on my birthday, or on a wintry day? And my classmates never asked me, obliquely or otherwise, when they heard my story. It was a girl called Delia who spread the news when her own mother told her what happened *all those years ago*. I was five or six years old, and for just a few days the object of gawking curiosity, even mild acclaim, because Delia's mother had also told her about another missing woman, one who'd flown across a deep and silent ocean and disappeared: Amelia Earhart, as free as air, a woman of heart, who had defied the laws of gravity in an ancient, juddering machine. Years later I would read about the objects washed up on a shore: a few items of clothing, some tools, a jar of freckle cream. I like to think these belonged to the fearless pilot, but there is no conclusive evidence.

Only Jimmy asked me how I felt. I remember it was nearing the end of our summer holidays, when we knew we would soon be parted. When we would attend different schools, no longer share our lessons and lunches, our leisurely walks at the end of the day, our schoolbags bumping on our knees, in time, as one. When I would feel his presence beside me, without looking: his black curly hair and dark brown eyes, his long, loping legs, which never raced ahead of me or lagged behind. When we would only talk because we wanted to. Like the time he told me that his dog was happy because it was always wagging its tail, but I insisted you couldn't tell if *all* of the dog was happy. Jimmy said that was *clever*. Another time, he said he looked forward to the future, because he wanted to be a kind and helpful teacher who let children laugh. But I knew you couldn't look forward to anything because, if the future hadn't happened, it would always be coming from behind you; you would have to look backwards to see what it was like. Jimmy said that was *very clever*.

We were playing cards on my verandah, drinking my father's homemade lemonade in the red, pounding heat. Jimmy leaned into me and said he had something to tell me but I mustn't breathe a word...How he'd stopped that morning at the door of his parents' bedroom, seen his father with no clothes on lying face down on the bed, and his mother *tugging the sheets around him with stiff and violent arms.* I'd never cared for Jimmy's mother, whose voice was like sandpaper and who liked to tell Jimmy and his sister they'd be the death of her one day. I was glad to have a father who spoke quietly, pleasantly, and who never used the word *death*, at least not in the beginning. But that moment on the verandah, when the sky was a tinny kind of paintbox blue and a kookaburra laughed from a tree, I told Jimmy I was sorry for what he'd seen. And then I asked him if he liked his mother. Because, sitting on the verandah, picturing her tugging at the sheets and scowling like a raincloud, it suddenly seemed important to know. Jimmy lowered his head and whispered that he *despised* her. Then he turned a blotchy red and told me he was sorry because at least he *had* a mother, and he was sorry as well because he'd never once asked me how I felt. How *do* you feel, he said, looking into the eyes that I once thought I'd stolen from my mother. I took his question, cradled it in my arms, felt its strange new weight, until my feelings loosened in my throat and finally came out of my mouth.

I asked him if his mother's face felt smooth and soft.

He said he didn't know.

I asked him if his mother ever talked about my mother.

He looked down at the ground, shuffled his feet.

I asked him what his mother had said.

He shuffled his feet again. Told me he'd forgotten. And then he mumbled that his mother was *very mean in her heart*.

I told him I already knew that.

There was silence and a sticky glass of lemonade in my shaking hand.

And then Jimmy stammered out his mother's words because I had asked him.

She called your mother crazy, he said. *Unfit to have a child*.

I remember the scene with a clarity that continues to unsettle me. The starkness of the white walls as I entered the room; the sunlight streaming through the window, lighting up my father's greying hair as he sat in his armchair, absorbed in a book. I can still see the shining blackness of his shoes; the bristles on his face: I stood so long in the doorway, watching, that I must have counted every single one. I remember his puzzled face as I approached him; the narrowing of his eyes when I asked him the question. Posed the singular, perplexing, beseeching word: *why*. I remember him putting down his book, deliberately, heavily, and the careful way he led me to the sofa. His knotted hands; the way he looked me straight in the eye. His shaking voice when he told me that my mother had been *unhappy* and *unwell*. He gave me these two words and set them down before me, like two heavy stones in an empty field. And then he sighed and told me that my mother had been *a very sad soul*. These were different words; they were the endless ocean waves drifting into shore, drifting out again, washing my mother away.

I waited, but he said nothing more. I waited. And then I pressed him further. *Why* was my mother unhappy? I said. And what exactly did he mean by *unwell*? The more he met my questions with his silence, the louder my voice became, the sharper my tone. Why, I demanded, why, why? But still my father said nothing. And then, finally, he clasped my hands and looked intently into my eyes. *It's very complicated*, he said. Then he released my hands, patted my head awkwardly, sadly, and called me his *wonderful girl*.

It was, I knew, less than satisfactory; it was, indeed, unfair. I began to think of my father as unfair. And as the weeks went by, I began to feel my anger as a knife that wished to hurt him, but which, because I loved him, plunged the blade into me as well. I began to feel guilty at the tensing of his body when I refused to meet his gaze; at the tremble in his voice when he asked me to perform the most mundane tasks – setting the table, passing the salt – as though he were afraid of me. At the way he reached out his hand to pat me on the head, and then hastily withdrew it, as though he had relinquished the right to touch me. A father and child unable to speak our feelings, bound in a frosty misalliance, with a terrible space between us.

And yet I could not abandon him completely, as I felt he had abandoned me, with his empty words and evasive complications. I never asked another soul, just as I never told a soul how Jimmy despised his mother. Even though I watched the faces of family and neighbours who must have known or might have known and even though I listened to their talk about everything and nothing, I never asked my burning question: please, can you tell me, *will* you tell me, why my mother went missing?

For months I would hear Jimmy's words in my head. We were childhood companions who liked to play cards, discuss the meaning of life, work hard at school, where girls learned to be ladies and boys learned to be men. And although we sometimes drifted back together, went to a few dances, discovered the art of gentle kisses, we never spoke of it again.

Nor did I tell him about the picture. How a girl in the library had giggled and nudged, furtively slipped me a book. How I'd seen the image of a hugely rounded belly and traced it slowly with my finger, as though I were blind, trying to find the hidden life inside. And how, over several weeks, I'd return to the library and study the drawing, until a prefect caught me in the act and snatched up the book, her face like a warning, snatching my mother away.

I should have been more prepared. I should have read the signs more carefully. The way my father began leaving me with Mrs Riley on Saturday nights so he could go to the cinema or have dinner with nameless friends. And then the one friend who came to dinner, and who my father introduced as Miss Blake. She was rosy and plump and smiling, and when she asked me if I was *Violet or Vi*, I tossed my head in twelve-year-old contempt, and again when she asked me about school and whether I enjoyed this, that and the other, all of us picking stiffly at our food. A week later, a picnic in Kings Park and more picking at food, more strained conversation. Miss Blake, I remember, wore a pale green dress nipped in at the waist, making her look even plumper and smoother, a woman content in her flesh, and my father buzzed around us, fussing over lemonade and sandwiches and was it too hot because if it was too hot we could move into the shade, until I wanted to shout at him to stop fussing and talking and playing at something I couldn't quite name, that I didn't want to name: this newness. And then a few days later, Mrs Riley asked me if I liked my father's *lady friend*, as though Miss Blake was different from his other lady friends: Aunt Jean and Mrs Riley herself and a few church ladies who continued to call for tea and scones, which they spread with cream and uplifting grace. And finally that moment at dinner: when my aunt raised her glass of sherry, told my father it was *high time*, and his face turned very red. And how, when she stared at him sternly and said, *It's been years, Herb, after all*, his face turned even redder.

The very next day, my father came to my room and asked if he might sit down on the bed and *have a bit of a talk*. His voice, I remember, was low and quiet, his face creased with apprehension, as he spoke of *an important decision...a special friend...giving some thought to getting married*. He must have seen the fear on my face, or perhaps something else that I didn't even know was there, because he dared to pat my hand, told me it was *now permissible* for him to get married. That the *right* number of years had passed. He told me I was *old enough and clever enough to understand:* that since my mother had never been found, she had been classified as *death in absentia*. It was, he said, a legal term. It meant that my mother was *dead in the eyes of the law.* I remember how I'd shuddered when he said this, as if the eyes of the law were looking down on my mother from an ominous, pitiless machine. And I remember sitting dumbly beside him, numb with a mess of emotions: diminishment, trepidation, resentment, anger; above all anger, that my father had finally brought my mother home in a heavy black coffin with his plump rosy special friend draped all over the darkly shining lid.

Are you happy with this? he said. *Because...*

I remember smiling grimly at his feeble words. I didn't scream or beat his chest, tear my hair out, run sobbing from the room, because he had, after all, taught me to be reasonable. Instead, I looked him straight in the eye, a stricken child needing to be cruel.

It's your life, I said, and shrugged, shrugging his happiness away.

Stepmother. It is a legal term that defines a woman as one's father's wife, and not one's natural mother. But in order to properly understand Millicent, indeed to honour her, we must return to the ancient origins of the word: the Old English *ástieped,* meaning *the bereaved.* A woman who has married a grieving man with a child, or children, not her own. For this, I would come to see, was Millicent's precious gift: her kindness to my grieving father, as well as to the daughter who didn't understand. My stepmother did not turn out the be the stuff of fairytale: cold-hearted, malicious, vindictive; she didn't cackle or have a wart on the end of her nose; she didn't murder her husband's child in a brutal imposition of power. Millicent was selfless, sensitive, she was unalloyed goodness, and she returned my father to life. For it was she, in the end, who told me *why*.

She told me some months after the wedding. This, too, I remember with a startling, almost preternatural, clarity. I was sitting on my bed, disconsolate, when, sensing a shadow at the door, I looked up to see this woman to whom I had been civil, if understandably remote. Just as I had been with my father; the three of us drifting on the surface of an ocean, unwilling or unable to dive into the wreck. I recall that Millicent wore a pale pink dress and a red-and-blue checked apron, and that her tiny feet were bare, as though she were on the verge of skipping from the kitchen and frolicking in the garden. I had never seen her without shoes before and, despite my resistance, I found myself surprised, even charmed, by the pinkness of her toes and her child-like feet. I remember how she waited at the door and how I continued to sit, silent and unsure, and how the loud ticking of the clock seemed impatient with her standing, my sitting. And I remember her voice, quiet, hesitant, asking if she might come in. Because she had something she wanted me to know. I nodded, watching her suspiciously, as she sat beside me on the bed.

At first her voice was halting, speaking of my father's love for me, his desire to protect me, always. And then she cleared her throat and told me that he felt he was to blame: for what had happened to my mother, as well as to me; that he felt he was to blame for everything. I felt my heart thump, once, a mighty burst in my chest, but I listened. And as she saw that I listened, her voice became steadier, more assured. She told me that, after I was born, my mother had grown restless, unsure of what she wanted in life, whether to have another baby or live somewhere else; how she began to cry over simple, pointless things like burning the dinner or forgetting to put salt in the soup. And how she couldn't seem to stop me, her baby, from furious hours of crying. *So you see, Violet*...Millicent drew in her breath. She told me that my mother had been unhappy, and because she was unhappy she became unwell. She couldn't make herself get up in the morning, not even to feed me, until she became so unwell that she couldn't feed herself. I remember suddenly seeing a picture: my missing mother, paper-thin and pitiably weak, and not seeing myself in the picture at all. And in all this time, Millicent said, my father felt confused and helpless and afraid. He pleaded with my mother, took her on sunny outings, bought her flowers and books and her favourite chocolates, made her tempting meals, read her stories as she lay in their bed. But because everything he tried came to nothing, because, in the end, he had no earthly idea what to do, he became impatient, even angry.

I remember how Millicent's voice had faltered, as it had in the beginning, but then she found the strength to continue. He felt so angry, she said, that he began to shout at her, and then finally he refused to speak to her, he shut her out, until he made her go missing. *Made her go missing.* She said it twice, and in the saying I could hear my father's voice confessing to his failure; how he knew he couldn't help my mother, felt he hadn't loved her enough, perhaps hadn't loved her at all. And how, after he had done everything in his power to find her, bring her back, return a mother to her child, he had failed her again. And failed his daughter. For the rest of her life.

Millicent's voice quivered, and for a moment I thought she might cry. But instead she did the unexpected thing, the lovely thing: she reached out, unfolded my arms and placed her hands gently over mine. Those hands, I recall, were warm and soft. Kind.

And so you see, she said, her voice now weighted with concern, *your father has been silent all these years because he thought he might lose you. That you, too, would go missing.*

I couldn't speak. Couldn't move.

She told me how much it had cost my father, to speak all these feelings buried in his heart. He had been shattered, she said, and she wanted to put him put back together.

Will you help me, Violet? she said.

Years later, I would acquire the word *depression*. I would learn about the ignorance of this condition in the past: the lack of diagnosis, the misdiagnosis, the blaming of the sufferer. I would acquire, as millions would acquire, knowledge and treatment of the symptoms, a medical lexicon to explain this shroud of darkness and how a person might be lead into the light. But in that moment, sitting on my bed, all I knew was *feeling*: for my mother and my father, and for the kind, loving woman who had wanted to explain. I clasped my hands in hers, tightly. It was enough, for the moment, for both of us.

That night, I went to see my father. He was sitting in his armchair, reading a book. He looked up, surprised to see me standing at the door, watching him closely. His hollow eyes, his pale face. And then, as I watched, I began to see what I could never have seen before. I began to imagine. I imagined him walking into a very different kind of room, where he spoke with a policeman, urged him, berated him, shouted him down in his fury. I saw him begging for information in the neighbourhood, in the next suburb, city, state, each question more frantic than the last. I saw him at his desk, writing pleading notices for the Personal Column. I saw him mailing desperate bulletins to the press, resting his head against the letterbox, barely able to stand. I saw him driving blindly, through tears, hoping that her figure might miraculously appear. And then I imagined him waiting. Waiting. I thought about the way he'd stopped saying his prayers and then lost his faith altogether. I thought about his longing for all that he had lost, and for all that might have been.

And so I walked across the room and stood before him. I told him I had something important to tell him, something pure and good and true. I told him I felt deeply sad about my mother, and that I had always loved him, would always love him. That I felt so cherished in his care.

And then he wept: as he no doubt wished he wouldn't; as I surely hoped he would.

My mother is the shape that sometimes hovers over me, the shadow behind a door, the faded letter hidden in a box: a jumble of metaphors that tells me I will never be able to find her. She is the future I cannot look forward to, because she is always so far behind me. But when I keep my eyes fixed firmly, lovingly, in the present, I can see her in my children: in Eliza's dark blue eyes and Milly's full, firm mouth; in James Herbert's strong, straight nose. And even though Eliza is impetuous and Milly inclined to be wilful, even though

James can never seem to make up his mind, they are all, like my mother, clever and sweet and shining with life. The three lucky charms she bequeathed me.

Last night, when the children were in bed and my husband was in his study, I watched the news on TV. I heard a woman describe another woman as *unfit to be a mother*. And even though the speaker's tone was entirely calm and measured, I sprang from my chair and threw my cup at the screen, crazed with indignation.

Oranges

If you were to ask me all about it, I guess I'd say it ended up with something really big but started with something really small. When Carly said to meet for coffee. Oh, and by the way, there was *this really cool dress* she wanted me to look at, just perfect for Jamie's party. *Look at.* Help pay for, she meant. Or *let's do a deal, Mum,* and I could pay for the lot. *The deal* would most likely involve doing lots of extra stuff around the house or doing her homework or, if she was desperate, getting As and Bs for her exams. She did that last year, when there was another *really cool dress* she wanted for the Year 11 ball. She'd ended up with straight As and a dress that cost five hundred bucks. Ted thought I'd gone completely nuts but I showed him the school report. *Another year like this,* I said, *and Carly's on her way,* even if I wasn't exactly sure where since she didn't seem to know, either. *She needs options, Ted, remember,* I said, parroting one of her teachers. More options than I'd had, anyway, only I didn't say that. I was nineteen years old when we married and I thought, well, this is it, here's the answer, only I didn't know what the question was. It was just a feeling, this weak-at-the-knees and fluttering feeling, and my heart swelling so big it filled my chest with wanting him. Well, we all know how long that lasts. Around six months, and soon my mum was telling me to be grateful he had a job and didn't get drunk or chase after other women.

I had that fluttery feeling with Carly, too, when I saw her little body held up in the air, saw her sweet, squashed-up face, her tiny hands like starfish. And when they placed her in my arms, how I felt we could go on forever, past all the stars and moons and planets and never stop. And then the bliss when she found my nipple, with her little hand resting on my breast. So I've kept those beautiful moments in a pocket of my heart and I open it up when things aren't going so well. Like when she talks back to me or slams her bedroom door. Never in my face, though. Or when she's slacking off at school. She's smart as a tack, Carly, but she can't always be bothered because school doesn't really do it for her, she says. I tried telling her once that school didn't do it for me, either, so I know how she feels. But she cut me off because no one, no one, she snapped, could possibly know how she feels.

So I was on my way to meet her and starting to feel a bit down, because malls are really depressing places. All the crap people buy and all the whining kids who get slapped down or ignored, that's the saddest part. I mean, I'm not saying I'm World's Best Parent or anything, but if you can't even be bothered talking to your kids why have them? But as soon as I saw Carly in the distance, waiting outside the cafe, I cheered up nice and fast. It's a funny thing, seeing your child from a distance, seeing them so grown and all separate from you. It's hard to believe you made them all those years ago, that they fitted inside you, safe and snug. She's 170 centimetres tall, my Carly, so you can't miss her, plus she's a knockout. Long dark hair and smouldery eyes, but she'll tell you she looks ugly. *My big ugly honker*, she calls her nose, and it didn't help when Ted said that lots of beautiful women had big noses and Carly said, *yeah, like name one, just one*, and he couldn't. *Cleopatra*, I said, kind of smug; I remembered that from school, how she was supposed to be the most beautiful woman in the world, how she was fire and air and could burn men up and they couldn't breathe without her. And *she* had a big nose, apparently. But Carly just shrugged, said that people had different ideas about women back then; *different aesthetic standards*, she called them. So as I walked closer and she was standing right in front of me, I was thinking, here's a girl who can say *different aesthetic standards* in one sentence and *big ugly honker* in the other. *Hi, Mum*, she said, wrapping me up in a great big hug. Two simple words and I felt it again, this warmth flowing out of me, the comfort of her arms. And how she must have wanted that dress pretty badly.

So we made our way inside and it was packed, mostly mums with toddlers jumping around or banging their toys or fists on the table. The occasional kid who sits like a statue. I never knew how to get Carly to do the statue thing. Anyway, we sat down and I saw him, this guy behind the counter who was waving at Carly and he was, well…divine. I mean, one of those men with smooth dark skin and a cutting kind of face, a dangerous mouth, actually *waving* at my daughter. *That's Nassif*, she said, *he always gives me an extra shot for free*, and straight away I was freaking out. My sixteen-year-old daughter who was probably still a virgin but what would I know, I was thinking, how could I be sure? And *always*? I mean, how long had she known this guy?

But it didn't turn out that way at all. I remember how Nassif gave a little bow and how his voice was thick as honey, all the women staring at him and wishing they were me. Carly told me later she reckoned lots of women bought coffee there just to *gaze in wonder*. She told me she got to know him a bit and, *no, Mum*, she said, all huffy and offended, *it's not like that*; she just liked talking to him. And, anyway, he was married with a baby, a brand new one. He and his wife came from Lebanon, not that long ago. I was glad she told me that because you don't like to ask, do you, the first time you meet someone. It always seems rude to me, a bit wrong, to say, *and where are you from?* It's hard not to sound like you're really saying, *aren't you strange* or *go back to where you came from*, when the truth is, you just want to know. I remember his accent as well, how his words were soft and sort of clipped at the same time. I remember his wide smile and his flashing eyes and the way he said my name: *It's so good to meet you, Eve*. Like I was the most important person in the world. And I remember what he said about Carly: *your daughter, she is very nice and very smart*, and her face was beaming because it wasn't her mum saying this but a very spunky guy who wasn't trying to chat her up. She told me once to *ease off with the positive-reinforcement stuff*.

She is very nice and very smart: so how could I not fall in love with him?

Carly told me what they talked about. How his English was getting better and how he liked to paint; not houses but people. He told her he hears music inside them and he paints it. And he told her about his wife, how she was young and loving the baby but a little bit alone because her family was in Sydney. And he talked about the baby. Carly said he did go on a bit but I just thought, well, here's another tick in a box: a man in love with his baby. Oh, and I nearly forgot, we went to look at the dress, which turned out to be not so cool when Carly tried it on. She said it made her look like a tart and I remember how pleased I was, her saying that. I mean, you should save looking like a tart for in private, for your husband.

And so over the next few weeks, Nassif and me, we got to talking too. Now it's not like I spend all my life drinking coffee and stuffing my face with jam doughnuts, because I work three days a week at a newsagency. I spend most of my time there checking and selling Lotto tickets by the fistful to the same old ladies and gents who don't know the odds and would be horrified if you told them they were gambling. So it was nice to sit in the cafe and have a bit of a look. It wasn't a sexual thing; well, maybe a little bit. It was mostly an aesthetic thing. His dark skin and flashing brown eyes, and the way he carried himself, upright and proud, even in that stupid cap. A dignified man, you know? So in between him rushing around tables and being sweet to all the women, he told me how much he liked the people here, so friendly, and the clean air, blue skies, the beaches. He came from Tripoli, where the beaches were…he held his nose, I remember, and laughed, only not like it was funny. He showed me photos of his baby and made me a picture with his hands, like he was cradling a tiny bowl. She has her mother's big eyes, he said, and his thick black hair and she is perfect. *Her name is Soraya, like a star.* An uncle in Lebanon had told him: *you must hurry now, you must make a boy*, and Nassif wasn't sure what to say. And I was thinking, *you wanted to say, get stuffed, uncle*, but Nassif found the word he wanted in the end. *She is awesome,* he said. *You know awesome? The barista, he say it all the time.* And somewhere in all the praise of blue skies and friendly people and feeling so lucky to be here, he told me how his wife missed her family in Sydney: an aunt, an uncle, three cousins. *But I want to come here to Perth, I put my foot on her,* he said. And there was something in his voice, angry and sad at the same time…well, it made me think it was better not to ask.

But Carly knew when I asked her. She gave me one of her *don't-you-know-anything* sighs. Like, didn't I remember the riots last year in Sydney? Cronulla? And then it came back to me: young Lebanese guys and young white Australian guys, fighting over women and the beach, about who owned Australia, I guess. Broken bottles and broken jaws and all those Aussie flags that suddenly looked really ugly to me. And I remembered even earlier, even uglier, in Sydney: the gang rapes by Lebanese men of *our girls*, Aussie girls, the hate mail and shock jocks and all the piss-off-out-of-my-country loony stuff. I was glad Carly was too young to remember that. Because she might know a lot more than me about history and the digestive system and infinity but there are some things…I mean, she's only sixteen. I remembered Nassif's voice, the anger and the sadness mixed up together. I pictured him rushing around in the cafe, working hard, keeping everyone happy. And I thought, well, he's just a guy who happens to be really good-looking; who happens to be Lebanese.

And then the next thing, the really big thing…it happened a few weeks later. When Nassif stopped by my table to show me the latest photo on his phone. But the baby wasn't just tiny anymore; she was this shrivelled little thing, a crumpled-up doll. Really skinny little arms and legs. A skinned rabbit, Ted would have called her. Nassif was looking at me but I couldn't say it, didn't know how to say it: *failure to thrive*. The words that don't blame mothers; the words that do. Then he started scribbling on a piece of paper, really fast. *Please, you come and see*, he said. *She has such beauty, you come and see*. He passed me the paper. *My phone, please, you call me, we make a time*.

Tomorrow, I said. It was as simple as that. Because what else can you do, really, when someone asks?

I remember putting on my seatbelt, wondering for the umpteenth time what the hell I was doing. I didn't know the first thing about the woman. Reem, her name was. What religion she belonged to, what she'd be wearing, whether we'd even understand each other. Or if my presents were the right ones. I'd settled for a book in the end, for when the baby was much older. *Hairy Maclary*, one of Carly's favourites. She used to snuggle up with me in bed, sound it out with me: *Schnitzel von Krumm with a very low tum*. And some flowers for Reem, purple lisianthus, because everyone loves flowers. So there I was, with a book and a bouquet, driving into the unknown. An outer suburb, they call it: *outer*, alright: left right out, with all the scrap-metal yards and used-car places with their tacky plastic flags, the heaps of grey high-rise flats with washing drooping over balconies. No wonder people turn to drink, and not a bus stop in sight.

And most of all, I worried about the baby and what to do or how to say things without making her mother feel mad with me, or less than who she was.

Finally I got there. One of those seventies houses, Toodyay stone and wrought-iron railings, a dry, spindly garden. Me walking up the cement path and feeling so nervous, so worried I might stuff things up, sensing a pair of eyes peeping through the blinds. And then the front door opening: a plump, girly face; huge dark eyes, almost black. She was wearing a green summer dress; so no burka or the other thing, no cross around her neck. Smiling brightly, letting me in; *come in, please, come in.*

'You are welcome in our home,' she said.

Slowly, carefully, like she'd been practising for days. I handed her the presents.

'For you and the baby,' I said.

As if they could have been for anyone else.

She hurried me inside, waving, waving, so pleased to see me, like a long-lost cousin, and her feelings were written all over her face, her body. The baby was nowhere in sight. I remember how Reem was really rapt by the flowers, buried her nose in them, scurried round for a vase, saying thank you thank you over and over, and then the book...well, you would have thought I was one of those three wise men bringing gifts to the baby Jesus. Everything seemed to make her happy, as we stuttered and stammered our way through words, did the dumb-show display with our hands. *Yes, baby sleeping now*, she said. *Only one*, I said, *a daughter, very tall*, and I stood up and raised my hands high above my head to show her my Carly. And I remember how Reem looked up at me and smiled, held up a finger. *One year in Perth*, she said, *here is good, good for all.* She didn't seem depressed. She smiled a lot, her voice was bright, the lounge room was spick-and-span. *And the baby,* I said, *she is…*healthy? Strong? Thriving? How much does she weigh? I didn't say any of this. I just drank my third cup of tea and ate a large slice of apple pie. *From shop,* said Reem, *I am sorry.*

And then I heard a faint whimper: an old, familiar sound. Reem startled and jumped up. What happened next will stay with me, always: watching Reem walk to the room, me trailing behind, watching her standing by a bassinet that was all decked out in pink. Seeing her so tight, as stiff as a board, and hearing the baby's cry getting louder, winding up. Reem lowering her arms into the bassinet, taking them out again, and then turning to me, frozen to the spot. *Come,* I said, and I put my arm around her, gently. Then I picked up the baby, this tiny, dark, howling creature, her arms and legs like sticks. I placed her in her mother's shaking arms, then pointed to my breasts, and she nodded, lowered her head. I guided her to a chair and the baby was still crying, wouldn't attach, nuzzled and groped like a blind little worm, slipped off and fussed and started crying again. So I held the baby's head carefully, placed her on the mother's nipple. And it happened. The gentle sucking, those wet little murmurs of contentment.

Reem looked up at me shyly. 'Is good?' she said.

'Yes, very good,' I said. Watching this greedy bundle, Reem's hand stroking her mop of damp black hair, I knew I wanted to say more.

'Soraya,' I said.

'Yes, Soraya. She is star.'

When I got home two hours later, Nassif sent me a message: *Reem call me say thank you for your goodness please come again.* So Reem could use a mobile phone but struggled with a baby at the breast. It was easy for me, I remember, but I reckon I just got lucky. We don't exactly carry them on our backs, do we, while we're working in the fields; pop them on the breast every now and then, keep on working. And didn't they tell her *anything*, show her anything, at the hospital? Give her the name of a clinic sister? I was shocked, I mean really slapped in the face, by what Reem managed to tell me in four cruel words: *Nurse say I stupid.* I had to stop myself from phoning right there and then. I mean, what stone-age cave did that *nurse* crawl from? Dark-skinned Reem, who doesn't look much older than a child. And so I shook my head, reached out my hand towards the baby. *You see? How happy?* I said. *Happy,* said Reem. *For all.*

And it was for all: for the baby, her mother and me. I'd sat down on the floor, tucked up my knees and given myself up to the sounds of the room: the softness of the baby's sucking, the occasional slurp, and a mother's steady breathing. I was in the moment, and I slipped back sixteen years, and everything made a lovely kind of sense.

I asked Carly what she knew about Lebanon. Nothing that Wiki doesn't, she said, and so we looked it up together, scrolled through lots of pages. We read about their *ancient culture*, so old it was happening before people started writing things down. And the language: Arabic. I didn't even know if I'd ever heard it spoken. And then the wars, a really long line of them. *Check out the latest one*, Carly said, *a civil war: 150,000 killed, 200,000 wounded, 900,000 displaced; it's mind-blowing.* She'd turned a bit pale, so I said let's look up Tripoli, where Nassif and Reem come from. So we googled it, ended up in Italy, tried again. Another mountain of detail about the ancient history and lots more about religion. *Mostly Sunnis*, I said, reading carefully, and Carly pulled me up. *Not sunnies*, she said, like Calvin Klein or Chanel, *it's Soony; the oo sounds like kangaroo.* We read about an island near Tripoli with forests, green sea turtles, all kinds of weird and wonderful birds, and I wondered if Reem had ever gone there as a child. If she'd pointed, all excited, when she saw those strange creatures, called out their names.

'Do you remember, Carly,' I said, '*our* special island? You ran around for days at Rottnest shouting *quokka, quokka, quokka,* just loving the sound of the word.' She thought that was *kind of neat.* And right at the bottom of the page, we read that Tripoli was famous for its orange orchards, and for *the fragrant scent that drifts through villages and cities.* It even had its own name, the scent, the word stretching out on the page: *Al-Fayha'a.* I tried to say it but I didn't have a clue how to. Carly said it looked kind of wafty, like the smell of oranges on the breeze. 'Like poetry,' she said.

And then she remembered the other Rottnest. They'd learned about it in history, she said, how thousands of Aborigines were shipped there; men and boys, locked in a prison, only let out to build roads and the lighthouse and so much other stuff, and hundreds of them died. She saw the question on my face: mostly disease, she said, and some of them were hung. I felt like she'd taken a glossy brochure and ripped it savagely in half. My baby.

I rang for a clinic sister to pay a visit. Not just any sister but my cousin Andrea's, who'd saved her life, she said. I only found out later that Andrea meant *really* saved her life because she was pretty close to doing herself in. She had five kids under the age of eight, her last one when she was forty. She thought she knew the ropes but she didn't, she was losing her grip on those ropes pretty fast, until Sister Ruby took her in hand. So this Ruby was a saint, social worker and friend, all rolled into one. Reem told me she was *a warm lady, in her eyes.*

It was easier after that, much easier, with Soraya. The crying, the sleeping. Amazing what a full tummy can do. I can't tell you how pleased I was, and relieved, because I'm not a social worker and I'm certainly no saint and it was great to see that skinny baby begin to get rolls of fat on her thighs and wrists, to see Reem smiling while she fed her. I knew what that look meant, the one that passes from mother to child: I've waited a long time to meet you and now you're here and the world is peachy perfect. And Reem made me laugh as well, when we talked about Nassif. *Very handsome*, I said, and she waved me to the bathroom, stood in front of the mirror and turned her head from side to side, primping and poncing at her reflection. So he was vain, her husband, and she knew it. And she surprised me on our shopping trip as well, when she saw all these celebrity magazines, how she whispered *everything is on outside.* She might have meant the breasts but I think it went deeper than that.

We sat in her kitchen while the baby slept and she showed me photos of her family. *Aunt, uncle, cousins. Sydney*, she

123

said. She shook her head and looked kind of dark. *Nassif say no Sydney*, she said. I remember how her face was suddenly fierce, much older. *Nassif is working hard*, she said, as if this might make Sydney go away. All I could do was nod. I looked at the photos for signs of what she might believe, who she might be, but everyone was in Western clothes, jeans and T-shirts, ordinary summer dresses. I asked about her parents and she told me they were dead. *Mother very sick, father in war.* Then she looked up with a smile. *But people like baby*, she said. She managed to tell me how people in the shops and on the street always asked the baby's name and how old she was, and how there was a man in the fruit shop who always said *g'day* and gave her really big oranges. *Like Tripoli*, she said, *oranges, very good*, and yes, yes, I said, as I watched her wave her hands like a breeze, listened to her say the word in Arabic. And it really did sound wafty. I saw it, too, floating along the streets, into houses, maybe into dreams.

Then her voice went all quiet and solemn. 'Many Sunni in Tripoli,' she said. 'We Christian. We come here, we not want trouble.'

I didn't want to be trouble, either, didn't want to make her remember things she seemed to want to forget. So instead we talked about other stuff, the stuff that makes you like everyone else. *Glasses*, she thought she needed glasses, *and so young*, she said. The washing machine that didn't spin that morning. And bathers; she wanted to buy new bathers because she was *fat from the baby*. She looked down at her breasts and laughed. When I was feeding Carly, Ted used to call mine *bountiful*, and I wondered what the hell he'd been reading.

Then one day, I remember, her face like a question, Reem shyly patted those bountiful breasts and asked would I please come with her to help her choose a bra. *Pretty one*, she said. And that was a good sign, too.

But she never wanted me to phone about the nurse, the one who called her stupid. She looked afraid and shook her head really hard. *No trouble*, she said, *we not want trouble*.

I remembered this as well: how it's always *we* for people like Reem.

So you'd have to say that things were turning out pretty well for Reem. But not for Carly. She'd been moodier than usual over the past couple of weeks. In fact, the happier I was the sulkier she was, and I started thinking maybe she was a bit jealous, that I'd kind of taken over. Or maybe she thought I should just mind my own business. The one thing I did know was that baby talk bored her to sobs. She'd get that glazed-over look whenever I talked about dimples and chubby thighs. And she snapped at me once, told me that maternal instinct was all a load of rubbish, that women were victims of a word I didn't know that sounded a bit like a hedge. Fair enough, I said, but why not see the baby anyway, in the cafe, so you can meet Reem and she can meet you. Carly was in a really foul mood that day, told me that the last part of my sentence was *redundant*. And then she pulled herself up: *the latter part*, she said, all sniffy and sure of herself. I was on the verge of saying *what's eating you today* but I put an arm around her instead. Waited. And sure enough, the tears came rolling down because she'd failed her biology test and the English teacher called her last essay *very disappointing*, which meant it was a pile of shit, she said, and of course it was shit; it was her fault cos she'd done it the night before and she didn't know what the fuck to do next year or the year after that or any year and she was so fucking useless, wasn't she? I ignored the language and just patted her back, held my tongue about making an effort because she'd already worked that one out for herself. And yesterday she'd been to see the guidance officer, who didn't guide her at all, she said, just told her a whole lot of stuff about being able to do anything if she put her mind to it. And had she thought about taking a gap year and what good would that do, Carly sobbed into my shoulder, just another gap in her stupid, pointless life. Then she cried a bit more, just petering out, and said sorry for the language and the waterworks and she'd come to meet Reem and the baby. *It'll get better*, I said, *just wait and see*, and she called me an eternal optimist. As if that was a bad thing.

So: that day in the cafe. Me and my daughter slurping banana smoothies, while there's this very cute baby being carted round by her dad, showing her off to the customers, mum hovering close, afraid he might drop the very cute baby on the head. All the regulars fussing and cooing. And best of all, how sweet Carly was to Reem, taking an interest, and not talking loud or slow, just normal. Even tickling Soraya under the chin, not quite sure, like someone must have told her that's what you do with babies.

And then the bad guy walks in and ruins everything. Only he didn't walk in; he was already sitting there, keeping an eye on things. Scowling. He was tired looking, and sour, the kind of guy who says every Christmas I don't know why I'm still alive and all his rellies are thinking the same thing. Anyway, the women in the cafe were having a good time with the baby, taking it in turns to hold her, trying not to flirt with Nassif, and then the old guy stood up and kind of steadied himself, put his hands on the table, and called out to Reem. *Hey, girly*. And there was something in his voice, something covered up, that made everyone stop talking, made everyone stare at him. *Hey, girly*, he said again, and Reem was looking all flustered and you could tell she'd heard it, too. The covered-up thing. She turned to look at Nassif but he was kind of frozen with the baby in his arms and then suddenly this man, this sour grey man lets out this stream of ugly words...*people like you...all your babies...we have to pay for people like you...why don't you go back...can't even speak the language...too stupid to even bloody try...*

And something inside me snapped and I walked over to this man who was really quite short and I'm pretty tall so I towered right over him. I wanted to tell him he was a complete dick and a fuckwit, but instead I told him he was cruel and ignorant and hateful and then I ordered him to leave. *Just get out*, I said. So he snarled and barged his way past Reem and out the door. I heard someone say, in a quiet voice: *What a terrible man*. I saw Reem's face, how it had kind of fallen in, how she looked, you know, just trodden on all over. Nassif was by her side now, the baby in his arms, holding them both. And then I saw my Carly get up, watched her walk over to Reem. She took her hand, leaned into her, gave her a gentle kiss on the cheek. And then suddenly everyone was coming up to Reem and patting her and saying things. And I heard it in their voices, what they were saying: the kindness. Quiet and low, like a bedtime song for a baby. The soothing sounds that mothers make, that everyone understands.

We didn't talk much, driving home. Reem kept cooing at the baby, who was starting to whimper; that I'm-getting-hungry sound. By the time we pulled up in the driveway Soraya was on full volume so me and Carly jumped out and helped with doors and parcels. We turned to go but Reem waved us in, all flushed with the baby's crying and wanting us to stay. *I make cake*, she said. So I fussed about with plates and knives while Reem sat down and put Soraya to her breast. And then it happened: Carly just sat up and stared. At a tiny, black-haired baby sucking at her young mother's breast. My daughter's face went all quiet, like she was thinking something for the very first time, like she was letting something go. I was on the verge of telling her she looked a picture but instead I just kept watching her watching the baby. Silent, all intense.

And when Soraya was patted and burped and told she was gorgeous and finally laid down to sleep, we started on the cake. *Orange cake*, said Reem, her cheeks puffed out, pleased with herself. *I make from man's oranges.* It was moist and melty and just a little bit tart, the way an orange cake should be. Carly called it *food heaven* and had two hefty slices. And I remember thinking: here she is, my daughter, who gets stroppy and moody and confused about her life but she's really kind and she's just knocked off a massive banana smoothie and now this cake so she doesn't have an eating disorder. And I thought how I must have done a few things right.

As we stood up to leave, Reem smiled at both of us. *I thank you so much*, she said, words bursting out of her, like you knew there was more she needed to say. *Your name, Eve*, she said, *in Bible*, she said. *Eve.* I couldn't help laughing; well, it was more of a snort, really, remembering all that rubbish from Religious Ed. The woman who ate the apple and caused all the trouble in the world. But of course I didn't say that to Reem. I'm not a Christian, Hindu, Muslim or a happy-clappy, but I believe in showing respect. Well, not to the happy-clappies; they're just idiots. And then she said it again: *Eve. She good woman. She make life begin.*

And after the hugs and the waves and squeezing into the car, weighed down with orange cake and light in my heart, Carly turned to me with the biggest smile. *You were awesome, Mum, in the cafe. I mean, really truly awesome.* And before I could say a word, before I could thank her or hug her or start to cry, she leaned towards me and took my hand. She'd decided, she said, about next year. *I'm gunna be an ESL teacher*, she said. *Help people learn English so they can settle in a new country and make a good life and tell stupid fuckers like that moron in the cafe to just bloody well fuck off.* I was just about to say *language, Carly*, but she beat me to it. *Yeah, yeah, I know*, she said, and gave me a kiss on the cheek. Leaned back in her seat. Did a deal: straight As this year and Ted and me could help pay for her language course. And maybe not charge her too much board because she wouldn't want to work too many hours at Chicken Treat; she'd need to really focus on her study. She used to call it Trick and Cheat, when she was tiny.

And that's when I had the feeling again, that feeling of being really alive. Only this time it wasn't a swelling heart or floating in bliss forever. I felt strong and solid and in the earth. I was a wall and you couldn't knock me down. I turned to look at my daughter.

'Thanks for being so kind to Reem,' I said. 'You were so sweet and sensitive and caring. You're a very good person, you know that?'

Carly gave me a dirty look. 'How many times have I told you, Mum? Go easy on the positive reinforcement.'

Self-reflexivity and Other Stuff

Another damned story about an eating disorder. It was the third one now. After she'd strongly discouraged them, not loudly but clearly: please don't write a story about a character with an eating disorder. She'd nearly said, *they've been done to death*. Instead, she'd warned them of the dangers of writing about this particular subject (as well as suicide, abortion and cancer): lapsing into sentimentalism or sensationalism, falling back on the formulaic and clichéd. She'd made this very clear to her latest bunch of the opinionated young, all of them keen to be writers and most of them averse to reading. What had that silly one said? The particularly vacuous girl with silver bracelets up to her armpits, offering her worthless opinions like flutes of champagne on a silver tray. *Oh, I never read*, she'd said loftily. *It destroys my creativity.* Or the other, marginally less silly one, who'd declared that reading inclined him to be *imitative*. The other students had raised their collective eyebrows at *imitative*, and Vanessa knew what they were thinking. Show off. Arrogant. Or, more likely, fucking prick. She still couldn't get used to over-hearing these expletives, as she walked down the corridors of the Department or scouted around campus in search of digestible food.

She remembered the plethora of *fucks* in the mall last week, waiting for fruit juice at one of those lime-green affairs staffed by emaciated adolescents with many facial piercings and depressing *joie de vivre*. Selling the type of juice that promised glowing skin, a healthy colon, spiritual transformation. How, standing in the queue, Vanessa had been forced to listen to the girl behind her talking on her phone about her boyfriend, who, it quickly transpired, was going to buy her a *fuckin' Armani pair of sunglasses with the fuckin' diamonds on the side, and, yeah, like of course they're fuckin' real.* Her boyfriend, it seemed, was not a *fuckin' tight arse.* Talk about the limits of one's language being the limits of one's self. She should have offered that girl a glass of Wittgenstein.

Vanessa remembered another student, Rebecca, who explained why she didn't read. Or, more precisely, why she had stopped reading – because she used to read *a lot.* It made her feel like giving up, she'd said, because she'd never be able to write *really good stuff like Alice Munro and that cool science fiction stuff like Philip K. Dick.* The class had, predictably, sniggered at the latter. How old were they, six? They were all at least eighteen, and there they were, carrying on about *dick*, like smirking children in the playground. And although she'd winced at Rebecca's *stuff* and *cool*, she was gratified to have a student who at least *used* to read and who appreciated quality fiction. And who, most importantly, had a sense of humility. That's what Vanessa wanted to say to her students, every single year: have some humility, for God's sake. You're eighteen years old and you know nothing, have experienced nothing, have read nothing, and you effing well want to write. But of course, she never said this. She was instead rational, temperate and instructive. She would always insist that we should read (mindful to use the inclusive *we*) because we can learn so much from the best writers. She would specify: we can learn about the different ways to use language, structure a sequence of events, deploy point of view, create a distinctive voice. And after giving them various examples, she would always conclude, rather lamely, that reading was also *a lot of fun*. Trying to use their language; remembering the course coordinator's words: *The students will complain if it isn't fun. Word will get around, and our numbers will fall like autumn leaves.* He'd actually said that, the pillock.

She returned to the eating disorder story, titled 'A battle with bulimia'. A hackneyed metaphor, the battle. It made Vanessa cranky. Who'd written this stuff? She flipped back to the cover sheet. Sophie Palmer. Sophie? Vanessa couldn't place her. And in a class of thirty-three students, she was hardly to blame. Five weeks into semester and she could only remember three names: Jason Chan, the *imitative* young man; Rebecca Riley, the used-to-read-a-lot young woman (an alliterative name was also a good memory jogger); and Daisy Picking, memorable by name and by astonishing beauty – tall, slender, with long black hair and almond-shaped dark blue eyes, flawless skin. She was the object of everyone's constant gaze. Vanessa knew the feminist theory about the curse of beauty but it came in very handy when you tried to remember a name. Thirty-three students, could you believe it? And the Department was worried about numbers dropping off! She wished they *would* drop off, like dead bloody sparrows from a branch.

She knew she must return, if wearily, to the task at hand. There were still twenty stories to mark, and they had to be returned by next week. When she'd first started teaching in this course – well, in reality, she'd been *dragooned*, because she was a writer. Of little note. Two stories published in literary journals, the last one ten years before, for heaven's sake – she'd spend at least an hour marking one story, until she surmised that many of the students had taken less than an hour to write them. And so, now…Sophie's opening sentence: *Because this story is so sorrowful and anguished and melancholy, like the hurtling, bitter drumming on a hard tin roof, the shadow of a life in all its terrible suffering, I'm afraid I won't be able to make it flow.* Merciful god, where did one start with this rubbish? Clichéd and excessively adjectival; mixed metaphors; redundancies: could a tin roof be anything but hard? And so clumsily self-reflexive, because someone must have told the poor girl that drawing attention to the act of writing was funkily postmodern. Who knew? And *flow*, for goodness sake. How many times had she told them not to use that word in relation to language or narrative? She had indeed expressly forbidden it, told them it was so imprecise as to be meaningless. *Flow* could refer to any number of things, she'd said: to rhythm, sentence structure, patterns of images or symbols, structure, tone. As a writer friend had once told her (a rather famous writer; in truth, more of an acquaintance than a friend): *Flow sucks*. Nothing quite like a dash of wit to get the message across.

That was another word Vanessa had tried to banish: *message*. Fiction doesn't have messages, she'd almost railed at her students. It is a form of writing that complicates our understanding of life; it raises questions rather than providing answers. Beware of those who think they have the answers, she'd insisted: the political and religious extremists with their dangerous moral absolutism, who know what's right and wrong, who know what's *good* for us. Trust creative writers, she'd almost shouted, because they want us to think for ourselves. She'd finally finished her declaration, exhausted, but at the same time proud of her lucidity and passion. And then, in the very next class, the astonishingly beautiful Daisy Picking had prefaced the reading of her story by telling them all it had *a clear message* that she *wanted to share with everyone*. Vanessa had beaten her metaphoric head against a metaphoric brick wall. *Message* was sufficiently discouraging, but *share* was simply odious.

Her friend Irene had given her *a message*, several times over, in fact. How Vanessa had become so cynical and jaded. How she reduced all her students to idiots. How she'd lost her capacity for pleasure and surprise. Vanessa had shrugged it off, as she shrugged it off now. If she'd been *writing* a story instead of reading all this trash (and when did she get the time to write anymore; they worked you like dogs in this place), she would damned well have written that she was cynical and jaded, that she had lost her capacity, etcetera etcetera, because she'd had such a miserable life. Not that she would ever write it, because in all likelihood she would *over*write and/or lapse into self-pity. Leave others to pour forth their gloom, she thought, as indeed young Sophie was trying to do on the pages before her, and which Vanessa had no choice but to endure.

She skimmed through the rest of page one: another *anguished*, and *unending tears* for variation. One *depths of despair* and a *comforting hug*. How on earth could she attend to the narrative when these impoverished words kept stumbling in her way? Of course the subject matter was important, but she had to assess their work on aesthetic grounds. This was a course in writing, not a series of therapy sessions; and, moreover, she wasn't a qualified therapist. (And why would she want to be? Forced to listen all day to the bleating of pampered neurotics and narcissists.) Vanessa checked the number of pages and felt even more dejected: this anguished *thing* must have been a good eight or nine hundred words too long. Well, not *good* words, any of them. Except for the odd preposition.

She stood up from her desk. Time for a cup of tea. Her niece had given her a selection of many different kinds of teas in a large wooden box. The geographical: English Breakfast, Irish Breakfast, Ceylon Orange Pekoe. The regal: Earl Grey, Lady Jane Grey, Prince of Wales. Tea to pep you up, calm you down, knock you out completely. It was like buying milk at the supermarket these days: low-fat milk or no fat at all, permeate-free, iron-fortified or calcium-enriched. And all the beans: butter, kidney, broad, lima, baked, mung, four-bean mix for the indecisive. Plus all the junk people heaped in their trolleys: chips, dips, fizzy drinks, jumbo packets of sweets. The last time she'd been shopping, a sporty-looking woman in tiny shorts had complained to her about the price of bottled water, as though it were all Vanessa's fault. And then she'd loudly denounced the chips and dips as the end of civilisation. *Diabetes, obesity, heart disease*, she'd said, a morbid incantation.

Now, *that* was an arresting sentence with which to begin a story: *Diabetes, obesity, heart disease, a morbid incantation.* Perhaps she could make a start, dash off a first draft, about the various illnesses of contemporary society, in a metaphoric sense, of course. Diabetes to suggest our insatiable appetite for the sweetness in life, our strenuous avoidance of suffering. She might even set the story in America, since the right to pursue happiness was, after all, enshrined in their Constitution, with all the rousing cheer of a fatuously grinning game show host. And obesity? A metaphor to convey the emptiness, the essential anomie, of the culture; over-eating as a desperate attempt to fill the emotional and spiritual void within. But that was someone else's argument: Susie Orbach's, she recalled. (She'd always thought *Susie* such an infantilising name for an influential feminist scholar.) And in any case, Vanessa realised, she had just used the expression *desperate attempt.* If that was the best she could do, how could she possibly write a half-decent story? It was worse than mediocre. It was…amateurish? Incompetent? Putrid? She couldn't find the right word, *le mot juste*, right here, right now. And finding it, she knew, was crucial. She subscribed to the Flaubertian dictum that *precision gives writing its power.* Precisely. Although Flaubert would have written that in French; and, unlike beleaguered academics, he had enjoyed the privileged time and space in which to search for all his bloody *mots justes.*

She decided to settle for *putrid.*

The one thing she *was* sure of, a belief that was set in stone, adamantine, was the potential danger of the auto-biographical. In her case, the autobiographical would not only preclude the necessary emotional and temporal distance required to write a competent story; it was also, quite simply, that the essentials had been written many times before. Not that *originality* as such was possible. She knew that all writers borrowed, pilfered, thieved, from other writers, with more, or less, awareness. This was even the case with writers who appeared to *make it new*: the modernist article of faith. The boldly experimental *Ulysses*, for example (first published in 1922), with its stream-of-consciousness narration, digressive structure, blend of comedy, pathos and tragedy, was surely indebted to Laurence Sterne's novel *Tristram Shandy* (first published in nine volumes, the first appearing in 1759 and the last in 1767. It was important to be exact.) And so, her story, Vanessa Sculthorpe's putative semi-autobiographical story, would hardly be an original; merely one of countless and often undistinguished romances employing the traditional plot of boy meets girl, followed by a series of seemingly insurmountable obstacles to the union and concluding in either comic or tragic mode.

What was the point, Vanessa thought, while at the same time thinking about the impossibility of rendering the process of thought: its incessant rhythm, its dissolution of the boundaries between the conscious and unconscious, the intrusion of sense perceptions impinging on the brain...*Did the world really need*, she thought...*Was it crying out for*, she thought again, *another boy-meets-girl? Boy ultimately sleeps with girl?* She thought not.

Lack of originality notwithstanding, Vanessa also knew that she would never write this story because its basic plot, albeit traditional, remained indisputably painful. That for years she had been trying to a-void the void that lay at the heart of her life. She also had to acknowledge that others might find it difficult, in all likelihood impossible, to believe she had once been a woman of considerable ardour who had suffered intensely, if relatively briefly, in her romance with Sam, with whom she had slept for eight deeply satisfying months. Vanessa paused. She had used the expression *slept with* before. An inadvertent repetition, like the reference to her miserable life. She always advised her students to read their work aloud in the interests of detecting, and thereby eliminating, any inadvertent repetition. Vanessa realised she had just used *inadvertent repetition* a second time. Or was it a third? This was, she recalled, another reason she had given up writing: this scrupulous but relentless self-editing as she wrote, such that she often lost the...she was tempted, for a moment, to think the word *flow* in her head. But *in her head* was a redundancy. And so: she was tempted to think the word *flow*.

Nevertheless, despite the burden of constant self-editing, it was important, indeed crucial, to thoroughly scrutinise one's creative choices. This was another matter on which she advised her students: that they should regard writing not as inspiration or the workings of the unconscious or as in any way spontaneous, but as a process that entailed constant drafting and re-drafting and re-drafting, world without end. That it was jolly hard work. And she would always end with a joke: *You don't have to be a good writer, but you must be a first-class self-editor.* Sometimes she would use *excellent* instead of *first-class*; or *fine*, or *meticulous*, depending on her mood. Always keeping in mind that these words were not, strictly speaking, synonymous. Which lead her to another piece of advice: never, but never (the repetition here being deliberate, the effect of which was to create an emphatic rhythm to evoke her sense of conviction) use a thesaurus. A thesaurus, she told them, is not always and necessarily linguistically nuanced or precise, and it rarely uses words in context. And context was all, after all. The context of social class in particular. (Vague foreshadowing.)

She still had far too many stories to assess. Miles to go before she could sleep. This one hadn't even put the tutor's name on the cover sheet, a practice that seemed to be happening more and more as the academic years lurched on. It didn't require too much effort, surely, to remember her name. Dr Vanessa Sculthorpe. Oh, she really didn't mind the occasional misspelling, and was only mildly peeved by the omission of her academic title, but she regarded the absence of her name as thoroughly unacceptable: a denial of her individuality, not to mention the devaluation of the professional expertise and experience that she unfailingly imparted to every single one of her predominantly ungrateful students. And it certainly did not predispose her to think well of this particular student, Dave Mills. She tried hard to picture him, but couldn't. His story appeared to be a piece of detective fiction, judging by the title: 'The case of a modern Sherlock Homes.' She sighed. Genre fiction: she despised its lazy plot lines, stock characters, one-size-fits-all assumptions. Ah, now she remembered. Dave. He was the exceedingly tall boy who always arrived late to class and had announced to an eager audience that *genre fiction sells*.

Vanessa had been awake all night, thinking; along with the obligatory tossing and turning, as well as the mandatory trying to come to terms with the haunting spectre of one's past. She had continued to think about the story she would never write, even if she were paid obscene amounts of money. Dan Brown money. J. K. Rowling money. For indeed it *was* obscene, raking in (if she might be permitted a colloquialism here to convey her sense of indignation) enormous amounts of cold, hard cash (another colloquialism for similar effect) to write complete drivel (ditto). Not that she had read any of those authors' works in their entirety, but the opening paragraphs perused in a bookshop told her all that she needed to know. The clichéd language for a start. A writer who used even one cliché was simply not to be trusted. And that, she would announce to her charges, with a final, teacherly flourish, is what writing is fundamentally about: making the reader trust you. Letting the reader know that she/he is in safe linguistic hands.

And so, back to the story she would never write. Nessie. Sam always called her Nessie, his Loch Ness Monster, when she was out of sorts. When she couldn't sleep with worrying that her family and friends would find out. Be dismissive of him. Look down their legal and medical noses: *a tradesman*, as though he were a child molester. Or, even worse, how they might *try* to be accepting. Tolerant. Damn him with their well-intentioned liberalism, oh-so-valiantly struggling to move beyond the category of social class as a measure of a person's worth. She used to lie in bed (twice now), Sam fast asleep beside her, imagining how they would describe him: *salt of the earth, man of the people.* Imagining what they'd say about her as well, but never, of course, to her face: So how did Vanessa ever snare such a good-looking man? No, here she must try to suggest their tone of voice with a simple typographical device: So how did *Vanessa* ever snare such a good-looking man? With her hooked nose and flat chest and very fat knees. Sam used to trace her nose with his fingers, lovingly. He used to cup her breasts, told her what his granny had once said: *Any more than a handful is vulgar.* And fat knees? He'd laughed out loud, and long, when she'd told him how she felt. *Nessie*, he'd said, *I don't stop making love to you once I get to your knees.*

And where, and how, did you meet, her family might ask. Almost certainly would. Because everyone wants an effing backstory. So, she would assiduously *not* write about the manner in which a highly educated if sexually unattractive woman from a respectable family, with all the material advantages life had to offer, found the occasion to meet a man who had left school at fifteen, had an alcoholic mother and a womanising father, who had got – no, not *got*, such an unattractive word – who was married at twenty, divorced at thirty, but *thank Christ no kids*, as he liked to say. (Interpolated snippet of dialogue to sketch in Sam's character.) This man who had never owned a suit in his life, who watched football on TV, scratched his belly, couldn't see the point of paying to eat in a restaurant when he could fry a damned fine chop himself. (Further details to suggest both his social class and his endearing understanding of what really mattered in life...although perhaps she was coming perilously close to perpetuating a middle-class version of working-class 'authenticity'.) How could she possibly write that she had been to someone's farewell party, drunken retirement send-off and all that, with the backslapping and flirting and no one flirting with her, no one even talking to her for what felt like hours, felt like a lifetime, when she'd had far too much to drink. And when, as an entirely predictable consequence, she'd become maudlin and self-pitying (but only in her head), and slunk off to a bar in another room. Saw a man standing at the aforementioned bar and walked up to him, as brazen as hell. *I'm a thirty-eight-year-old virgin*, she'd said, *and I want to have a fuck.*

That was a terrible line, a line from the script of a B-grade movie. Well, at least she'd retained enough of her critical faculties *not* to say: *And I want to have a fuck before I die.*

Reflecting on the preceding paragraph, Vanessa noted a distinct if subtle shift in style, from the formal to the more colloquial, from grammatically complete sentences to a combination of fragmented and extraordinarily long sentences. All of which suggested a breakdown in her usual reserve, such that her writing effected a transition into something approaching interior monologue, as she approached the heart of the matter. The desire to have a fuck. Her auspicious meeting with Sam. Not too bad, really. Quite promising. Perhaps, after all, she still had the knack.

And so, to continue:

Sam had laughed, put an arm around her, told her she'd found just the right man. And she had, for a while. Until she drove him away. But *driving* was a completely inappropriate metaphor, not to mention (sigh) an overused one. She'd put poor Sam in a coffin, instead. Not literally, of course; she'd never *actually* shot him or plunged in a knife, or even poisoned him slowly with the arsenic in apple pips. She'd read about that somewhere – this wifely method of poisoning an inconvenient husband – in some gothic short story, the name of which she'd forgotten, but which she would google. (How much easier for writers these days, to have this world of handy, sometimes arcane, knowledge at their lazy fingertips.) But no, she hadn't used a gun or a knife or apple pips to destroy her Sam. For in the end, what (non-literally) killed him was a word. (Surprise, surprise.)

After eight months together, when Sam had expressed some consternation that he still hadn't met her family, Vanessa had told him that her family, her parents in particular, had *standards*. He'd given her one dark look and walked out the door, leaving her no time to explain her thoughtless linguistic choice. Her ultimately cruel inability to find *le mot juste*. She had told him, more or less implied, without meaning to, not for a moment – no, good heavens no – that she was ashamed of him. When what she'd *really* meant was... they would make him feel uncomfortable; they wouldn't recognise his very precious worth.

He never gave her the chance to explain her intended meaning.

She remembered how one of her students had written, at the end of their story: THE END.

Vanessa returned to the marking, because there was nothing else to be done. Now it was a story about a decline into depression, if the opening sentence could be said to provide a clue: *Carlotta was depressed*. She flicked to the last page: twelve pages, which made it substantially over-length. So both bulimia and depression, it would appear, had failed to adhere to the guidelines: *works that are substantially over or under 1500 words will incur a penalty*. The students either hadn't read this instruction or simply didn't care. In any case, she could always fall back on the tried-and-true formula for assessment, the appropriately professional routine: begin with words of praise and encouragement; follow this with some suggestions for improvement; end by summing up the whole and wishing them all the best for their future endeavours. So: *Carlotta* – no, that was the character's name – *Edwina, you are to be commended for tackling such a socially important issue… There are some pleasing aspects to your story, such as…However, the writing might benefit from some judicious…*No, no, erase that one, since the poor girl wouldn't know the meaning of *judicious*. Vanessa finished her comments, rapidly, and confidently assessed the story as a C minus, which meant that Carlotta, no, Edwina, might just scrape through the unit and proceed to the completion of her dubious degree.

What Vanessa had wanted to write, if she only had the choice, if she wasn't restricted by civilised niceties as well as bureaucratic codes, was this: *Don't waste your time, Edwina, or mine, trying to write, until you have done some extensive reading, and until you have gained a more complex experience of life.* But as she hauled another story into sight, Vanessa knew, if she were really honest with herself (implying her admirable capacities for self-reflection and self-criticism), that she had no right to offer this advice. Because she had known Sam for only eight months; and although she had read, over several decades, veritable container ships of books, she had to admit that the rest of her life was nothing. Nothing. (The effect of using a deliberate repetition here was self-evident.)

And then she remembered the writer Henry James who, by all informed biographical accounts, had never had a single sexual experience in his life. Except for those few hours he'd spent lying in a narrow bed, trembling and afraid, side by side with Oliver Wendell Holmes (a far less well-known and well-regarded writer), burning up with longing, unable to move. This particular scene had been depicted in *The Master*, by the Irish writer Colm Tóibín. (A superb novel that had not yet entered into the literary canon; it was surely only a matter of time. But then, Vanessa thought, wasn't everything? Only a matter of time?) So: Colm Tóibín had written an exquisite scene – unbearably tense, unutterably sad – about nothing happening to a man as he lay next to another man; a man for whom nothing would happen in his entire life. Not in a sexual sense, that is, for *what happened* was always in the head with Henry James. He had made a luminous career writing about the tortuous nature of consciousness, the refinements of fine sensibilities, the moral ambiguities of life. Vanessa was reasonably confident that he'd never walked up to a man in a bar and declared that he'd never had a fuck.

She managed to finish the marking in a week. Unlike some of her colleagues, who *rocked up* to meetings (that was long-haired Giles, a relic from the sixties), with their marking incomplete. Her bell curve was looking decidedly misshapen: two As (begrudgingly), seven Bs (slightly less begrudgingly), fourteen Cs (mostly magnanimously), ten fails of varying degrees of ineptitude. She would have failed more of them if the regulations allowed it. (Was the word *it* grammatically necessary?) As it was, she would have to artificially inflate the scores to meet faculty requirements. She would be, as always, the first to arrive at the meeting, and the first to leave, closing the door behind her. She always suspected unambiguous, as well as thoroughly unprofessional, character assassinations. Her highly un–collegial colleagues would no doubt be calling her *punitive, mean-hearted, arrogant*. With a flat chest and fat knees to boot. (*Knees* followed by *boot* was, she knew, unfortunate.) As she walked down the corridor, Vanessa began to feel a tightness in her chest (a rather lazy way, she had to acknowledge, of indicating a turning point; at least she hadn't stooped to *suddenly*). She clutched her folder to her chest, suddenly dismayed. Were they right, after all? She certainly never *intended* to be punitive or mean or any of those other damning epithets they almost certainly proclaimed behind closed doors. (In actuality, one door.) She was always diplomatic in her comments, even if her heart wasn't in it. But that is how others saw her, and had no doubt always seen her, ever since her arrival in these hallowed halls. (A deliberate use of a cliché to indicate her mockery of this august institution. Another cliché.)

Eight months of sexual satisfaction, and one word to end it all. (Unexpected reference to the past, to suggest how she continued to be haunted by it. The workings of the subconscious, and all that palaver.)

Vanessa knew there was more, much more, to their eight-month relationship than sexual satisfaction, and she knew why she always left out the details in her head. It was easier that way. It was better, it was gratifying, indeed empowering, to be able to change the story of her life, to make it more endurable, since she couldn't change her nose or breasts. Unless she had surgery, of course. Nor could she change her knees, unless there was some complex medical procedure known only to a few devotees of radical self-fashioning. She looked down at those knees, remembering. Sam. (Another haunted-by-the-past moment.)

147

It had been a trying afternoon. Three of her students (not all at once) had rapped loudly on her door and more or less (she was inclined towards *more*) barged into her office, demanding a re-mark of their work. Two had complained they'd been unfairly penalised because Vanessa had mis-counted the number of words. One story, she remembered, was far too short; the other far too long, *diddle diddle dumpling my son John.* (She was pleased with this jaunty rhythm; a deftly comic touch.) The third, and final, source of grievance was a plagiarism issue. The student had steadfastly main-tained that she hadn't *pinched* anything. Vanessa read out the offending unattributed quotes, and, in each case, named the author and the text. *The roar that lies on the other side of silence.* George Eliot, *Middlemarch.* (The student claimed she had never heard of him.) *It was the best of times, the worst of times.* Charles Dickens, *A Tale of Two Cities.* (Even philistines who attended that cultural abomination known as the Quiz Night knew the source of that opening sentence.) *One day I will find the right words, and they will be simple.* Jack Kerouac, *The Dharma Bums.* (Just because she was, in her students' eyes, antediluvian, didn't mean she was stuck in the world of nineteenth-century fiction; she could recognise Kerouac when she saw him, sunglasses and all.)

And indeed she would take her cue from this Amer-ican writer of ostensibly spontaneous prose – which was later revealed to be the product of extensive re-writing and whose chief stylistic contribution to English literature appeared to be the elimination of the full-stop in favour of using long, connecting dashes, such that the phrases between those dashes created the illusion of improvisational jazz riffs or some such, a practice characteristic of his Beat phase and not his Buddhist phase and who cared, really, about all this soul-searching and spiritual journeying and where did it get him in the end? Dead from internal bleeding due to long-term alcohol abuse – Yes, she would listen to Kerouac and find the right words, the simple words, at last. She would take her linguistic knife from her academic bosom and stab the malcontents, the unread, obtuse, semi-literate, extremely ill-mannered students (and in one case, a mendacious one) barging into her room (she no longer had any need for *more or less*) with their sense of entitlement emblazoned on their spotty foreheads:

Fuck you! she would shout. *Fuck the lot of you; fuck you all. Exterminate the brutes.* (Joseph Conrad, *Heart of Darkness*, but only the final sentence.)

But Vanessa knew she would never shout, even mutter or whisper, these simple but nevertheless existentially confronting words because she was far too well-bred.

And she was vaguely concerned that this was rather an abrupt ending.

Exploring

Maggie

She's just come back from her weekly shampoo-and-set but she's *not happy with it, not happy at all.* Like saying it twice makes her seem more important. Presiding in her *villa*, as if she's in the south of bloody France. Picking up her cup with that annoying little crook in her finger.

Sometimes I pretend she's a TV set with the sound turned off.

'There's *another* new girl in the salon,' she says, 'and I can't tell you—'

But she does. How she was drenched with water all the way down her back, not even an apology, and now look at her hair, just look, so dry and lifeless. Don't they train their apprentices these days…some basic courtesy wouldn't go astray…and they've put up their prices *again*…

She lets out one of her end-of-the-world sighs.

'How was your lunch?' I say. 'Miss Maud's, wasn't it?'

'It was decent enough,' she sniffs, 'although there was too much dressing on the salad. And Beryl *did* go on about her arthritis. No backbone, really, never enough backbone.'

I hint that the bones might be the problem but my mother's already moved on. 'And at the end of it all, there was such a commotion,' she says. 'When I stood up from the table and fell to the floor, and so many people came rushing, fussing about. Did I want some water? Need a doctor? Honestly, you would have thought I was dying.'

'They were only trying to help, Mum.'

'And when I stood up and shooed them away, one young fellow it was, he called me *a game old girl*. I mean, what a cheek.'

'It was a compliment,' I say. 'And it's an oxymoron.'

'What's that?' my mother says, suspiciously.

'Well, it's like a contradiction, but it makes sense if you think about it some more. You're, well, you know, getting on in years, but you're as sprightly as a young girl.'

'I see.' Carefully smoothing her dress over her knees. 'Don't call me sprightly, Margaret,' she says. 'It's condescending.' She waits, raises an eyebrow. 'You didn't tell me that Judith won't be here for Christmas,' she says. 'She came round yesterday to fix my radio and confessed she was taking a trip. With a friend.'

It's Jude, not Judith. I've given up trying to tell her.

'A friend called Lindsay,' my mother says. 'I've never heard of any *Lindsay*.' She shakes her head. 'Taking a trip with a boy? At her age? I mean, I know young people do things differently these days, but—'

'Lindsay's a girl,' I say.

My mother looks mightily relieved. Oblivious to the fact that young gay people do things differently these days.

'Judith tells me they're driving to Melbourne,' she says.

'Yes, it's a road trip. Across the Nullarbor.'

'The Nullarbor? You mean, the desert?'

'Correct. The same one we drove across in my last year of primary school.'

I remember my mother's moaning all the way across that bloody desert, with Dad listening to the cricket and me sulking in the back seat, missing my friends. *A family holiday*: deeply ironic on both counts.

'Another one of your father's ridiculous ideas,' she huffs and puffs. 'He said you could find yourself in the desert. Well, I said, *I don't need to find myself, I'm not jolly well lost.*' She tosses her newly coiffed head. 'All those miles of nothingness,' she says. 'Just sand and sky and that long black road. I thought I'd go quite mad.'

'I found it a spiritual experience, actually,' I say.

She never has a clue when I'm pulling her leg. It's what Dad used to say. *Your mother could have ten legs and she still wouldn't know.* She takes a genteel sip, sets down her cup.

'And how long is this *trip*? Exactly.'

'A month.'

She shakes her head again. It's a wonder it hasn't fallen off. 'I do worry about your child, you know,' she says. 'She should be buckling down, thinking about her future. At least finishing her degree. First history, was it, and then changing to whatever it is she's doing now—'

'Psychology. It's the study of people's minds and how we behave. *Why* we behave as we do.'

'Well, how does that mean anything? And how's it going to get her a job? It's just as useless as history. And now this *trip*. Not even home for Christmas.' Her strategic pause, before moving in for the kill. 'A firm hand, Margaret, that's what she needs. If only you'd—'

'I'd what? Made her go without dinner, or given her the strap? Tied her to the bed?'

My mother stands up briskly. 'I'll make a fresh pot of tea,' she says. 'There's no point discussing this when you're in one of your moods. And watch out for that cup, will you? It's Moonlight Rose, the last piece in my set.'

It's 6.47 when I finally make my getaway. Exactly forty-seven minutes of that flinty stare, checking out my lipstick (too bright), my skirt (even brighter), and my brand new strappy red shoes. Forty-seven minutes of her whining and judging, with her pinched grey mouth and the grey walls behind her and the grey fucking carpet as well. I tug hard on my seatbelt, muttering *why the hell do I bother*, why do I drink all those bloody cups of tea, force myself to phone once a week to make sure she hasn't keeled over in the shower and dropped dead, trying not to wish she had. *You're such a horrible person, Maggie. Really. And you should stop talking to yourself.*

I used to hope a grandchild might change things. That when my mother saw my baby for the very first time – her pixie face, the smoothness of her skin, those tiny fingers like twinkling stars – she might finally surrender into love. They say it can happen like that, how love can skip a generation. But she didn't even want to hold the baby, or stroke her downy head. And from the start it had to be *Grandma*. You could hear the capital letter in her voice.

As I pull out onto the road, I picture Jude's bright-eyed face, feel her arm around my shoulder, the warmth of her hugs. And I wonder for a moment if my mother ever longs for it, alone in her widow's bed: the everyday miracle of touch. Oh, I know it's easier to be kind when I don't have to look at her, listen to her everlasting groan about life and her *sit up straight, Margaret, you're developing a hunch* and *you're leaving already; why are you always in such a hurry?*

And now the supermarket will be closed and there's not a thing to eat in the house except those salty cheese-and-onion biscuits that have you up all night drinking jugs of water. Everything's shut by six o'clock except the deli. Another thing about the place that drives Jude crazy, along with all the money talk that fills up the news, after the local-police round up: the odd home invasion or mugging, as if sleepy old Perth's the Crime City of the World.

She told me I'll find her lying in a ditch one day. *Died of boredom* tattooed on her chest.

And now this road trip. I try not to think about it, but of course you do, even after all these years. Her father driving to the hardware shop to buy a washer. I should have let that tap go on dripping. I should have held him in my arms and whispered: *Don't go, not yet.* Just a few minutes, even one more minute, and he would still be here beside me.

Jude

I'm preparing for Grandma cos that's what you need to do. You don't see her for a while and you forget and then two minutes in her company and you're going demented. Every time I see her, Mum goes up a hundred points in my estimation. If Grandma had written the Ten Command-ments, there would've been fifty or a hundred: *Thou shalt not come in with those boots on…Thou shalt not waste your money on…Thou shalt not gobble your food…Thou shalt not pull a face like that; if the wind changes, you'll stay like that forever.* That was the killer one. I was six or seven when she told me that. It's what's called *a defining moment,* when you're a kid and you realise that adults can be incredibly stupid.

So as I'm pedalling along, I'm hoping I can get this done in a hurry. Two light bulbs to change, that's easy, but a bunged-up sprinkler could be tricky. Grandma asked me once how come I can do all that stuff. The manly stuff, she means. And I wanted to laugh into her face: *it's because I'm a lesbian, Grandma.* But that would scare the bejeezus out of her, and would only make life harder for Mum. I can just hear old Grandma now, how Mum produced *a monster,* or some other bullshit like that.

Lindsay. It's only been a couple of months but it already feels perfect. It's not just the sex, although that's *really* perfect. It's because she's so damned nice. Not all sugary and girly pink, just always seeing the good in people, being positive all the time. Like, I've never heard her say a bitchy word about anyone – even the bitches who deserve it. And she's smart as well; I mean, I would never go for a dumb girl who can't think past the clothes in the mall. She cares about the state of the world and the poor fuckers who make up most of it. And as I'm pedalling along I'm thinking of that night she asked me what I thought of her bum. We're lying all wrapped up and exhausted and she asks me what I think of her bum. Only she said *backside. So what do you mean?* I said, and she went all kind of shy. Did I think it was too big? *Too big for what?* I said. Anyway…and that was our first really serious talk, I guess, about us. About how I didn't want a girl who was always carrying on about the way she looks, fishing for compliments and feeling insecure all the time. It's such a turn off, so pathetic, although naturally I didn't put it like that. And what I found out was she'd never been with a girl before. So she told me all about these two guys and how they both told her she had a big arse. I mean, get real. Sometimes guys can be so…so not evolved. And I remember saying to her, is that why you're switching to girls? Trying it out? Like I was an experiment. And that's the part where she really blew my mind, I mean, made me feel so amazing. She said she'd never been attracted to girls before but she fell in love with me. *So when did you start*, I said. *Falling in love with me?* And she said she never really started; it just grew kind of slowly, all the talking we did about our families and friends and politics and stuff and it all came creeping up on her so she had to take my hand, she just had to, and kiss me.

So when did you *know?* she says. I said I was about fourteen, and then I told my mum. Lindsay was just so amazed but she hadn't met Maggie then. I mean, I don't take this stuff for granted. I know kids whose parents have gone apeshit when their kids told them; these ignorant dudes who couldn't stand the thought of having *one of them* for a child, and then the suicides and depression and stuff. It's awful and sad and just so wrong. And now we've got these Christian loonies running the country who tell us being gay's a sin, an abomination in the eyes of the Lord, and who make people sick and go mad, locking them up in detention centres for years, sending them to countries with no human rights. And they reckon they're so full of compassion. *We're saving lives at sea*, they carry on, banging their bloody self-righteous drums, the Minister for Immigration and his band of Merry Christian Men. Maybe there's a woman or two, but you have to look bloody hard. 2013: the first time the authoritarian State apparatus allowed me to bloody vote, and look who's ended up in power. Thinking they're always right. Only that's not thinking at all. It's like, the refugee issue; it's not gunna go away by locking people up, it's a global problem that's gunna take thinking people to solve it. I mean, you gotta start with the causes: poverty and war and government corruption. You gotta start exploring the issues.

Lindsay agrees with all of it. Only she's been thinking she might vote informal next time cos she's starting to feel disillusioned, like it's hard to trust the pollies anymore. That really freaked me out and I told her: there are people in other parts of the world prepared to die to get the vote, so you just gotta exercise your right. Mum's a bit like that, I have to say; she reckons we're all pretty much powerless. But that's just so defeatist, I said. Like what about people power? Collective action? *Oh, yeah*, Mum said, *fat lot of good that did, millions of people marching to protest against the invasion of Iraq and the pollies didn't listen.* I said, *I don't remember that*, hoping to wriggle out of it, and then I came up with my trump card, how people do it differently these days, mobilise through social media. Egypt. Tunisia. Iran. So Mum had to say I had a point. But I'm kind of glad she didn't know about the ones that didn't work. Belarus. Thailand, a few years back, all those tech-savvy people occupying Bangkok until the bloody military cracked down on them. So, OK, it doesn't always end up right, but you have to make a beginning. You have to keep believing.

So I'm finally here at Grandma's block of *villas*, like she's in the south of bloody France. That great big lawn with an invisible sign that tells you to keep off. It's for lawn bowls but I don't think Grandma plays, she's not the kind of person who bends. And everything else is grey, the walls and the bricks and the blinds, and everyone has a mini garden in front, all clipped and neat. Nothing's more than ten centimetres high, I reckon. Just shoot me when I get old, if it means being stuck in a place like this. So I lug my bike up her steps and lean it against her wall and I'm thinking, she's probably gunna jump out and say: *Thou shalt not leave your bicycle there*. I ring her doorbell. No answer. Try again. She's usually really quick to come to the door; maybe she's worried the person might have second thoughts and take off. I press the doorbell again and this time she opens, and she's the same as always. Grey all over.

I steel myself, follow her inside and she points to the ceiling light.

'I suppose you need a chair,' she says, like it's my fault I'm not Gulliver in bloody Lilliput. And then she sits down to inspect me at her massive jarrah table with fifty million legs; I mean, who ever comes to visit her? So I screw in the light bulbs and she doesn't even thank me. I tell her: *I'll check the sprinkler; I'll leave you to it, Grandma...*So I fiddle around with the damned sprinkler for a bit, try the water, nothing's coming out, try again. I figure it needs an expert. Then I have to ring the doorbell again cos she's shut the door behind me, like a thief or mugger is gunna slip in while I'm working in the garden.

She opens the door and shoos me in, says she has something to show me. *Look, Judith*, she says. It still drives me nuts that she doesn't know my name – or won't use it, anyway. There's a fat, spongy book on the table and she makes me sit down while she turns the pages, pointing. *All my bow*, she says, and I'm thinking, what's a *bow*, and then I get it: boyfriends, that's what she means, she's showing me these photos of all her old boyfriends. All in black and white, with these tiny little triangles on the corners so the boyfriends can't escape. Reginald, a policeman, she says, quite high-ranking, but her father thought he was *too rough around the edges*. Well, he's big enough to have a lot of edges, I'm thinking: the guy's bloody massive. And now it's someone called Arnold…he cycled in the Commonwealth Games, she says, her voice going all mushy, *such lovely ankles*, and I'm trying not to crack up. And then Geoffrey, a bank manager, *very important, but he had an accident, poor fellow; was never the same again…*This weird kind of sideshow, all these guys stuck on the page, peering out from another time. *And here's your grandfather, of course*, and her voice goes all sniffy. I've forgotten how good-looking he was, kind of chiselled in the face, and I'm thinking how Grandma must have been a bit of a minx in her day, but I've never seen a photo of her when she was young. She's always looked this way to me: grey and cold and full of anger inside. And I'm just about to ask her if she's got a photo of herself when she starts sniffing again and I can't believe it: she's crying. Trickles running down her cheeks, really small and slow.

'There was one I loved, *really* loved,' she says. 'But I don't have a picture of him anywhere.'

It's like watching a movie and she's one of those old-time movie stars in close up, the ones that make you laugh when you're watching TV stoned out of your mind at two in the morning. Only she isn't really funny. She's kind of sad. And then she lets out this great big sigh, coming from deep inside her.

'Walter Raleigh,' she says. 'The explorer. It was our little joke.'

Eeeechhh...All sorts of images are running through my head, ones I don't wanna see. And then the doorbell rings and I jump up. Know I'll have to answer it, with Grandma sitting all weepy at the table. And there at the door is a really snooty looking woman I've never seen before.

'Ah, the grandchild,' she says, like I've just got out of prison. She places something in my hand. 'Your grand-mother's glasses case,' she says. 'She left it at my place this morning.' And she's looking me up and down, inspecting me, from my stubbly hair to my denim shorts, and I see it in her face: where are the sweet young ladies of yesteryear, with their frills and ringlets and rosebud lips? She's looking at me kind of funny, sort of cross-eyed or squinty, and then I see something else as well; I remember what Mum called her: *Widow Bligh with the odd glass eye.* Mum gave her that name, *to help keep me sane*, she said, whenever she's *condemned* to have afternoon tea with her and Grandma. So now I can tell Mum I've seen it with my own eyes. There must be millions of jokes you can make about this...condition. Which isn't really funny; I mean, the old dear could've lost it in some terrible accident, spilt acid or something. But I'm trying not to laugh anyway and Grandma's calling out: *who is it, Judith, who is it?* I thank Widow Bligh for her trouble and close the door qui-etly. Cos even if I have stubbly hair and wear denim shorts and I'm gay, I'm an old-fashioned kinda girl. Polite. All my mother's work, cos my dad died when I was really little.

Grandma's still sitting at the table, looking at her photos, still pointing.

'Just look,' she says. Kind of spits it out. 'Just look at your mother.'

Mum's in a really short dress and she's got great legs. Her hair's all loose, down to her waist, and she had this come-on kind of grin, one hand on her hip.

'She looks cheap,' says Grandma.

'She looks amazing,' I say. 'Like a singer in an all-girl band.'

Maggie

She finally opens the door. Ready for yuletide battle in her best beige jacket and skirt, beige shoes and stockings. In forty-degree heat.

'I haven't seen you for so long I thought you were dead,' she sighs.

'And seasons greetings to you too, Mum.'

I must keep my cool. I haven't even walked through the bloody door. At least the food will be worth it. She knows how to roast and bake with the best of them. Always makes a brilliant trifle for Christmas, with glittering, quivering layers of jelly: lime green, gold, ruby red, and peaks of ivory cream. I used to watch her when I was a child, her pained expression when she cooked, her hands all martyred and stiff. And yet she makes these things of beauty: her trifle, her cheeky cupcakes dotted with hundreds and thousands, steak-and-kidney pies with delicate frills around the edges.

I register that she's staring.

'What's that thing you're wearing?' she says.

'It's a sarong. Perfect for the heat.'

'Well, there's more of you outside it than in.'

'The table looks lovely, Mum. The silverware is positively blinding.'

Prune-faced cow, I think, and trail into the dining room.

'Did you find a new salon?' I say. 'Your new style looks… well, flattering.'

She pats her head, says she's *quite pleased* with the new girl. *She's not too bad*. Praise so faint it's invisible. She barely glances at my gift – the usual hamper of shortbread, jams, English breakfast. When it comes to Mum, they say it's the thought that doesn't count. Then she hands over the usual voucher for me, from David Jones this year, *to buy yourself a decent dress*. Ok, she's already had two goes at me: I'm a neglectful daughter, and I look like a slut. I should start keeping count, see if she can beat last year's tally of sixteen insults over one bloody meal. Then see how long it takes me to stop holding my tongue. Two minutes, so far. I hold my tongue as we sit down to eat.

It's exhausting, this tongue-holding business, cutting the turkey, dabbing our mouths with her best linen napkins. And now she's starting up about Jude, wondering why on earth she wants to bother with this trip.

'She told me she was going to *hang out* for a while when she gets to Melbourne. Hang out *what*? I said. And it always rains in Melbourne. Always. It doesn't sound like *my* idea of fun.'

I wonder what her idea might be, as I try not to listen to her banging on about Jude being so foolish, wanting to drive all that way, then the dangers of driving at all in this day and age, all the young hooligans drunk and speeding, you see it all the time on the news. And innocent people getting high-jacked in their cars.

'High-jacking is for planes, Mum,' I say. 'It's car-jacking. And you're thinking of other places. Like Johannesburg.' I wouldn't dream of telling her what I see in my dreams, even in my waking hours: Jude's terrified face as a car comes roaring towards her. The horrifying crunch of metal, the pools of blood, the shattered limbs. Jude promised she'd call or text every night but I insisted every second night would do. And I didn't moan and groan about *how can you abandon me at Christmas?* She asked if I minded and, *of course not*, I said, *not a bit*. I didn't want to make her trip a guilt trip, after all those years my mother's been laying it on me with a trowel. But I *will* miss our debrief: the post-Christmas laughs on the drive back home. She does a great imitation, my daughter, of her Grandma's pursed-up mouth, her frosty voice. It's really funny, and it isn't. It's enough to make you weep, if you cared to.

'Johannesburg.' My mother's voice brings me back. 'I remember,' she says. 'It's where all the *black* hooligans are.'

Just shoot me, I think. Just take your gun from your holster and shoot me in the heart. Sneak up behind me and drive a pickaxe through my head. But she's done with *the blacks* now, it seems, unless she veers back at some point to *the natives*, with their crime sprees this and government handouts that and *they don't know how lucky they've got it*. She's moved on to the state of my house, and have I even *noticed* the sagging hallway ceiling; it could fall down at any moment. I have a sudden vision: my mother standing in the hallway, crushed, buried alive, as white flakes of plaster drift sweetly to the floor.

She's straight out of Dickens, I once said to Jude. All those comic-grotesque characters. Jude gave this some thought, and then said, *yeah, with a bit of Lady Bracknell meets Lady Catherine de Bourgh. Snooty, as well as empty inside.*

I pour myself another glass of wine. My second and last, because I'm driving. I offer my mother another glass but she's always been a no-thank-you-one-is-quite-sufficient kind of drinker, as she places her respectable hand across the rim of her Waterford crystal. I watch her tight face across the table, and my father's words come back to me. *A fine-looking woman,* he called her. His Dorothy-never-Dot. And I saw the wedding photos once: her long, graceful neck, high cheekbones, a tiny waist, but shapely, too. She was already thirty when she married, thirty-five when she had me. Pretty unusual. And having only one child, even more unusual back then. I used to wonder about all that but then I stopped. There was no point looking for the life inside her, since she never cared a jot about mine. I study her eyes, her pale, cold blue eyes that never see me, and I feel myself sinking in the chair. I am the child she might not have wanted. She's the mother I just can't bear. And here we are, staring at each other across a table full of gleaming cutlery and gold-rimmed plates.

Merry bloody Christmas.

You disappoint me, Margaret, she said. I was four years old and I can't remember what I'd done or hadn't done, but I remember her looming face and that thin bitter mouth and how she waited, waited for me to lower my head but I didn't.

You disappoint me. And she told me every day by the hardness of her face.

'Why are you looking so glum?' she says.

Glum. Fucking *glum.* Try wretched, Mother. Try angry and hurt. I had a father and a husband who loved me and left me. I have a mother who never leaves me at all.

She leans across the table.

'You have so much to be grateful for,' she says. 'I know you lost your husband, too, but at least…'

I feel a horrible taste rising in my throat.

'At least what?' I snap. 'At least I have food in my mouth and a roof over my head and…'

'You had love.'

My mother's voice is quiet and her face is beginning to twitch and, for just a moment, I think she might start to cry. But then she pulls back her shoulders, tells me not to slurp my wine and to jolly well sit up straight. And she's back: the captain of her mighty ship, who'd melt an iceberg in a hurry. And because I won't defend what I'm wearing, because my mother almost cried, because I'm tired and confused and bored all at once, I stand up from the table. Announce that I'll do the dishes. I hear her voice behind me, demanding to know how I'm spending Boxing Day. Since she's not busy herself. I put the tap on full blast, run the water fiercely.

As I scour and scrub, rubbedy-dubbing my mother away, I remember this morning, when Jude put Lindsay on the phone. The girl I first met a month ago. I asked her to call me Maggie but I could see how it stuck in her throat. Not that she's prim-and-proper, just super polite. Always asks if she can take a shower or make a cup of tea or take an apple from the fridge. It took me a few days to get used to seeing them together: the adoring looks and holding hands, the stroking. But now it feels, well, normal. The affection. It's what I had before Tomas died; what I miss most of all.

We miss you, Maggie. That's what Lindsay said last night on the phone. She called me Maggie, and together they miss me. The trip must be going really well.

Jude

The trip across was great, sharing the driving and all. There was this hilarious moment where Lindsay's driving along that long straight flat line and we hadn't seen a car for ages and then all of a sudden we hear it: this siren. And then we see it coming towards us, the old flashing blue night. So Lindsay pulls over and this cop gets out of his car; he doesn't look a day over twenty, looks like Justin bloody Bieber. Anyway, he saunters over and takes out his notebook and it's *Miss* this and *Miss* that, is she aware that she was speeding? One hundred and twenty kilometres per hour. Is she aware that the limit is 110 kilometres per hour? And Lindsay's all *no officer, of course, yes, I'm sorry, officer*, and all the time she's doing the fluttering damsel routine, the batting eyelashes and simpering smile. So the cop tries to sound all gruff, which doesn't really work if you have a baby face, and then he lets her off with *a warning this time*, and a timely reminder that *speed kills*. So we wait until he drives off and we're cracking up laughing. *Female empowerment!* I shout, *And you didn't even show him your tits!* So Lindsay pulls up her T-shirt and shows me and we're both hysterical with laughing cos I think we're just so relieved we didn't get slapped with a massive fine. And then we take a breath and get stuck into the Maltesers again, even though we've eaten so many we both feel kind of sick.

And then sleeping in cheap, grotty motels, it was part of the adventure. Not that we had money for anything fancy but it was kind of cool, anyway. The first one had a bedspread with these huge purple flowers and there was this puke-coloured carpet and a lamp in the shape of a pineapple. Seriously. We'd lie on the bed and look around and just laugh at the goddamn ugliness of it all. And have sex. There was something really cool about that too; the secret. The old guy at reception saying he only had a double bed and how we'd just have to take it or leave it. I reckon it must be easier for girls cos most of his generation, they don't think about girls having sex, like, it would never occur to them. But guys…I mean, two guys in a double bed, that's bound to make them suspicious, 'specially in these Hicksville motels.

And then when we were driving, that moment when we both had the same idea: let's turn the engine off and jump out of the car and listen to the silence. It was so, so dark, there was this huge black sky and this eerie kind of nothing all around us, and we held our breath, both of us, and it was like we were the only two people in the world. And then we waited some more, kept really still, and I swear I started to feel like I couldn't tell the difference between me and the sky and the road and the silence, like I wasn't even there any more. The ineffable, that's what it's called; something that can't be put into words. I wrote that on an essay once and the tutor wrote all these comments, like I *should try to employ a more analytical vocabulary. The ineffable: an experience that exceeds or transcends language.* There we were, me and Lindsay, sharing the experience that exceeds or transcends language, when she suddenly lifts her arms up in the air and shouts: *we are the new explorers.* And I remember thinking that was neat, how she was having a good time, but this other part of me was feeling a bit…annoyed. That she was making her mark on a sacred kind of space. I don't mean I felt Indigenous or anything, that would just be arrogant and stupid. It was just that her words broke the silence and kind of broke the mood. This great big calmness I was feeling inside me. And then I looked at her, standing under that huge black sky with her long blonde hair fanning out in the breeze and her face all shining as she was looking up at the stars, and I let it go. But I did feel kind of ambivalent.

And now I'm remembering how I forgot to call Mum; it's been three days and she'll be getting worried, I know, even if she hasn't sent an SMS. She's probably been having nightmares about accidents and stuff. She never says it but you can tell by the way she looks whenever I ask to borrow the car. I mean, I've been driving for nearly two years now and I've never had an accident, not even one small dent in the car. But I totally get why she worries, my dad having been killed in a car and all, he swerved so he didn't hit some random dog running across the road. Mum said she was only glad the dog was a stray so she didn't have to get angry with the owners, letting their dog go loose like that, or even feel sorry for them. It was, like, seventeen years ago but I guess it must always be there in a pocket in your mind, or your heart.

She's had a few boyfriends and they all seemed OK; not loud and trying to impress, cos that's one thing I really hate about some guys. And girls as well: the listen-to-me-and-I-don't-give-a-stuff-about-you brigade. But not one of them ever stayed overnight and they pretty much disappeared as fast as they came onto the scene. I asked her once; it was after my graduation and she put her arms around me and said my dad would have loved this moment. I asked her why she'd never hitched up with anyone again and she kind of laughed and said it was all a bit too much effort. How she liked her own company, anyway, and having the two of us together. Only she didn't say it like she was owning me or smothering me or expecting me to stay with her forever. She just said it like she loved me.

So when we pull in at our last motel I call her right away. She tries not to sound all relieved and just wants to know how everything's going. So I don't tell her about Lindsay speeding, of course, or how she shouted out in the ineffable space; I just act all kind of vague and say we're having a good time. And then I remember: Grandma. I completely forgot to tell Mum about the Walter Raleigh guy. So I try to make it real for her with all the details and Mum's going, *no, no, you're kidding me...I would never have believed it...* And at the end of it all I say I reckon it's kind of sad, Grandma and her long-lost love. There's this great big silence at the end of the phone, and then Mum says, almost snaps at me: *there's always a detail to make a monster seem human.*

Maggie

I'm just so relieved she's back home. In one piece. Alive. It sounded like the drive over was fun but then coming back was pretty tedious; I mean, how could it not be? And it doesn't sound like the trip went all that well in the end. Not that Jude said as much, but she was lukewarm, I have to say, not glowing and excited like she was at the beginning. That's what she's telling me without telling me, as we sit on the front porch trying to keep cool, trying to cut down on the air con. Tough it out when it's still thirty degrees at ten pm. We've become so damned soft – not just Jude and me, I mean everyone. I even read in the paper about these people who leave their air con on all day while they go to work because they want their house to be arctic as soon as they step inside. I mean, I know it's *their* stupid money but it's *my* precious planet. Mine and my daughter's and all the other daughters and sons. The neighbours always have their air con blasting all day, all night, and now they're blasting away with André bloody Rieu again. I hear Jude say, *fucking André Rieu again*. And then she turns to me, her face a bit furled up with worry, and leans forward in her chair.

'I have a sort of question for you,' she says. 'It's…like, you won't get mad at me, will you? Last night I went into your bedroom. I mean, I wasn't snooping around or anything, I was just looking for your nail clippers and, well, I opened the drawer of your bedside table and saw your wedding ring and…I've never seen it before. I wondered if…'

'Yes?'

'It made you too sad to wear it.'

I draw myself up, remembering. 'The ring…it got too big for me, love. I lost so much weight after your dad died, and it kept slipping off my finger. But I didn't want to size it, you know, have it made smaller, because our wedding date's engraved inside the band.'

Jude looks at me kind of softly. 'So you never put it back on?' she says. 'The weight, I mean.'

Does a body change to fit a different life? Diminished.

I tell her, no. That I just got lucky. She gives me a tiny smile.

'You could wear it, you know…on a chain around your neck.'

I nod. 'I used to do that, but…well, it's been years, love. Now I'm happy just to look at it from time to time. It's enough.'

Jude picks up her mug, cradles it in her hand. Wants to know if she can ask me something else. Like, how did I know that her father was *the one*.

I have to laugh. Tell her again that her father was a very kind man and a lot of fun and he loved her, his baby girl, to bits. But I'm not sure I believe in *the one*, I say. Because I think if you can make a go of it with someone, stay together for a long time, it doesn't prove you've found your soul mate. It probably means you have certain qualities that would help you make a go of it with any number of people. Jude wants to know what sort of qualities, and so I rattle off a list of virtues: patience, being a good listener, respect for the other person, a willingness to compromise and to talk about your feelings, being able to laugh at yourself, a sense of perspective, being supportive.

'Bloody hell,' Jude laughs. 'Show me where I can find that person.'

And something in her voice, a smudge of defeat, makes me wonder if things with Lindsay might be worse than I thought. And because my daughter reads me like a book, she gives me a shrug; tells me they're having a few problems. I don't want to patronise her. I don't even want to give her advice. So all I say is that people in a relationship often see things differently; that's normal. But it's *what* you see differently that matters. I can hear myself sounding patronising. Just keep talking with her, I say. Giving her advice.

'Sexual relationships can be the pits,' she says, and then gives me a wide grin. 'I'm thinking of switching to animals.'

'Jude!'

'No, seriously, there's this guy, a philosopher called Peter Singer, we read his stuff at uni, and he reckons that people should be allowed to have sex with animals. Because all animal species are equal.' She's on a roll now, telling me. 'So Peter Singer says we can have sex with animals as long as we don't exploit them. You know, be cruel to them, or even just use them for your own pleasure. The animal has to enjoy it, too.'

Talk about a new idea. Well, to me, anyway.

'So how would you know that the animal enjoyed it?' I say. 'I mean, apart from the involuntary physical response.'

'Easy,' says Jude. 'The animal would light up a ciggie afterwards.'

We laugh together.

'So here's the real question,' I say, teasing her. 'What kind of animal would you choose?'

Jude gives this some thought. 'Maybe a giraffe,' she says. 'I've always been attracted to creatures with long, graceful necks.'

'Make mine a bison,' I say. 'I like an animal who's big and hairy.'

Jude leans back in her chair. 'Changed my mind,' she says. 'I'd go for an anteater, with their really long tongues. Or…I know, a lapdog. Did you know that, in the eighteenth century, women used to have these little fluffy dogs and they'd get them to burrow under their skirts and—'

'Now that's really gross. Please, enough.'

'You started it,' she says, and pokes her tongue at me.

Jude

I feel like I need the ocean so I can have a bit of a think. It shouldn't be too crowded cos it's not that hot today, for a change. The first day under forty for how many days now? It's some kind of record. So who says climate change isn't real? The stupid government, that's who. Well, they say they believe in it and then what's the first thing they do when they take the reins of power? Abolish the Ministry of Science. Like they can run the country on religious faith. Well, they're already doing it; one of their loony Christian MPs making some link between abortion and breast cancer, and only paying schools for counsellors if the counsellor's a priest or a cleric or something so they can sneak in some Christian propaganda on the side. Imagine one of those dudes trying to counsel someone gay? Like, they'd be telling them it's OK to be gay as long as you don't act on it. I mean, that's so unjust, and one of the most hateful things you could ever say, even though they reckon they're all accepting and loving – we're all God's creatures and bullshit like that. And they're not even properly trained, no qualifications; but, hey, they've got some hotline to the Almighty, who'll tell them what's right and wrong. And as for...*Jude, calm down. You're meant to be calming down*, I say to myself. Look at the ocean and feel calmer, *make yourself a little bit of peace inside*.

I was gunna ride my bike but then the pedal came loose and so I had to take the bus and wait a whole half hour. Public transport in this place is bloody awful, just lamentable. Buses running late and half the time the trains aren't running at all. No wonder there's so many cars on the road. And what's the solution? Build more fucking roads. Lindsay called it *disgraceful*. And as the bus is rattling along, I'm thinking about the two of us. How it started out so well when we first got to Melbourne. Staying in this share house in East Brunswick with my old friend Remy. Five students in the house when they're only meant to have three people – but they can't afford it otherwise, the rent's so ridiculously huge. Especially for a place that's a demolition job, all the holes in the walls and the sagging ceilings and a bathroom you had to close your eyes in, it was so full of the kind of grot that needs an oxyacetylene torch to lift it off. Lindsay was cool with it all, though, she even thought it was fun. The girl who lives in one of those McMansions and her parents have a cleaner and a gardener who comes every week. So I guess East Brunswick was her idea of slumming it.

We had a good time just hanging out, though. The Queen Victoria Markets and the beach at St Kilda and walking around the Botanic Gardens, which was really neat cos Lindsay knows a lot about plants and flowers, even the scientific names, cos her dad's a botanist so she grew up talking about it. So that's a *meaningful* thing to talk about, I said, and she nodded. *But my parents never talk politics*, she said, *it's like it doesn't matter to them cos they're so comfortable.* And she's right, I guess; like, her mum doesn't even have to have a paid job. I just couldn't imagine my mum not working, I mean, she didn't have any choice. Even if she likes her job. Only sometimes it depresses her, being a social worker: all the human misery, she calls it, and sometimes she says that social workers just can't win. They get blamed if some poor baby with druggie parents dies, and they get blamed if they take the baby away.

So the bus is nearly there and I see some really beautiful girls in bikinis and tiny shorts walking along the road. Someone told me once that Australian girls are the most beautiful girls in the world but I wouldn't know cos I've never left Australia. And then I remember Lindsay having a go at me for staring at girls. I mean, we were walking along the street, on our way to catch a tram to the National Gallery and she makes me stop and says she *just can't bear it any longer*, the way I keep looking at other girls. Sounding like a melodrama queen about to have a fainting fit. Telling me it was so *disrespectful* of her. Well, I kind of brushed it aside cos the tram was coming, and so we got in and didn't say a word. But then it got better once we were in the gallery cos it turns out Lindsay knows heaps about art – the history and all the different perspectives and brush strokes and things that I'll have to look up to remember. Look up and learn.

So it's all going well again, until I see her. Ginny. She's peering at a painting and I know straight away it's her cos she's still got that chopped-up flaming-red hair and she's as hot as ever. And it was great, seeing each other after all this time, two years I reckon, catching up. Ginny's studying law in Melbourne, I mean, half the student population of Melbourne must come from Perth these days, and while we're talking I'm making sure that Lindsay feels included. I know what that feels like, when people are yakking on about the good old days and you're standing there all kind of alone, wondering when the hell they're gunna stop. So at the end me and Ginny have a big hug and we say goodbye and it's all fine. But then I get the treatment from Lindsay. *So, one of your old flames, I suppose.* Old flame? Like she's living in the 1950s. And then she's wanting to know all about us: how long we were together and was I in love with her and on and on she goes, in the middle of the gallery, and I'm thinking, *this is so not good.* This is disastrous. She's prying and jealous and possessive and I'm not liking this at all.

And so I told her. I told her I was starting to get seriously annoyed. And then I said, *Lindsay, we have to go somewhere quiet and have a serious talk.* So we took a tram back to the Botanic

Gardens, neither of us saying a word again, and we sat in the shade of a big old tree with some long Latin name, and once we got past the tears and the saying sorry, we talked. She said she only wanted to know about my past cos you can't really know someone just in the present, and I said it was like she was trying to *own* my past; like I wasn't allowed to *have* a life apart from her. And she said that's not true, she completely accepts that I've had other relationships but...and then it started coming out: how she believes in one relationship at a time and she's worried that I don't and I said I want some freedom and she said that's not freedom, that's dismissing her feelings, *her integrity*, she called it. And so on and on we went, round and round in botanical circles, bringing up all sorts of stuff about our values, what we want, how we treat other people. The big things, like Mum said. And in the end, we made a kind of pact. That when she's around, I'll stop looking at other girls. And I'd tell her if I've had sex with someone else. *And not before?* she said, as though I'd be planning it. As though these things don't just happen sometimes. *They don't just happen*, Lindsay said. *You always have a choice.*

So as the bus rounds the corner and the ocean's right there, blue and bright and startling, I'm thinking how we sort of agreed to disagree. That we'd stay together and see what happened next. Because we do care about each other. I know that for sure. She's smart and beautiful and she's this funny kind of mix I've never known before, like timid and shy one moment and then giving me an earful the next. Unpredictable. I remember how Mum told me once how she and Dad used to fight quite a lot, but they always came back together cos in the end they knew it was worth it. They'd been living together for years before they decided to have me. And as the bus is lurching to a stop, I'm thinking about her. Mum. How she's been alone for all those years. I mean she's had a few guys but no one ever serious, she told me. And she said she's not lonely. Being on your own doesn't mean you're lonely, and being married for years doesn't mean you're happy. *I mean, look at Grandma*, she said, *married for ages and every day must have been a misery*. I remembered looking in Grandma's bedroom once, when I was a kid and Grandad was still alive, and I saw two single beds and two bedside tables with a prim lace doily on each one. I was too young to understand what that was all about, but I remember how it made me sad, just looking.

The bus stops and I thank the driver and he says, *no worries, love*. No worries. When did people start saying that all the time? And *not a problem*. Me and Lindsay have this game now, we count the number of times people say *not a problem* when they serve you in a shop or a cafe. Laid-back Perth; nothing's a problem. The relaxed and comfortable city, like a giant bloody Ugg boot.

I wait forever to cross the street cos there are millions of cars and just about every one only has the driver sitting inside. I finally get to cross and walk to the top of the embankment, stand perfectly still for a moment, trying to take it all in. It's always the moment, when you first catch sight of it, this bird's-eye view. The huge stretch of sand, the ocean that looks like it goes on forever. And all the people: half of Perth must be there, in the water and leaping about, sun baking like idiots. Melanoma Central. Where do they all come from? Doesn't anybody work anymore?

The beach, hey? I remember that Cultural Studies unit I did, where we talked about the role of the beach in the

Australian psyche. On the beach, said the tutor, no one knows if you're rich or poor, a mining magnet or a guy who cleans the toilets. He called it an egalitarian space. I mean, do tutors actually get paid to spout crap like that? So how does that work when you leave the beach and climb back in your BMW or your rusty old Falcon? Buy your stocks and shares or take a trip to Centrelink? I was gunna say something, using the language you're meant to use, about idealised cultural myths, self-serving conservative concepts of national identity, but someone else got in first and then everyone was talking away and so I just sat back and thought, again, so what? Yackety yackety yackety yack, just get off your arses and bloody do something. Like all those petitions people are always posting on Facebook. *Hey, I signed some petitions today, protesting about this and that, standing up for that and this, and jeez I'm such a good person.* Let me put my compassion on display. Bunch of tossers. I'm gunna stop going on Facebook.

I walk down the embankment and take a seat on the grass. Look at all the tanned mums and dads sipping their chardonnay, with their cute little kids prancing all about, and I can look at the girls now, too, can't I? I'm trying not to listen to the chatter all around me but I just can't help myself, it's so compelling in a horrible kind of way. Like whose swimming pool's being re-tiled and whose kitchen's having a makeover. A makeover? Most places in the world don't even *have* a fucking kitchen. And check out this really skinny woman sitting just down the slope from me...she has so many visible bones it looks like she lives on three lettuce leaves a day...carrying on about her neighbour having lipo-suction for those *last few kilos she hasn't been able to shift.* And now she's on about *her disaster of a nanny* caught smoking in front of the children. And, yes, a very hot summer; but, oh no, this climate change business is complete rubbish, absolute rot, scientists getting big fat grants to peddle lies, not a shred of decent evidence. I want to stand up and shout at them all but I know it wouldn't do anything except make me feel better for ten whole seconds. It's like when I shout at the TV news, which always makes Mum laugh or sometimes gets her goat. But then I remind her that I *do* stuff as well, like hand out how-to-vote cards and go on demos and even door-knocking last year, in the leafy suburbs with their Federation houses and two BMWs parked in the driveway. I made up a joke about my door-knocking, which she thought was pretty funny:

Knock, knock.

Who's there?

A volunteer for the Greens.

Don't pollute my porch with your left-wing propaganda.

So I reckon I'm entitled to shout at the lard-arsed, well-heeled pollies who want to smash the poor, the pensioners, the disabled, and all of us living-by-the-seat-of-our-pants students.

I try to block out the noise around me, and in my head. Try to calm down. Mum says I'll have a coronary before I'm twenty-one. So I focus on the ocean, breathe in deeply, breathe out. Breathe in, breathe out. Some people pay good money to be reminded to breathe in, breathe out, and— here I go again, thinking about the stupidity of the world; so I try to settle again, keep looking at the ocean. And as I'm looking, seeing the shimmering blue and the awesomeness of it all, I'm liking the way it makes me feel so small in a good kind of way, and how it takes me back to Lindsay and the desert. The vast, ineffable space she must have felt that time even if she was shouting and kind of spoiling my mood. That's what we need, all of us, to be reminded of that space, get put in our goddamned place. Just be a bit more humble, you know; remember how we don't really matter. Except we do, we're the stewards of the planet, and we have to take care. Release ourselves from patriarchal attitudes to nature, like we own it and can rubbish it all we like.

Patriarchal attitudes to nature. Another little catch phrase from uni. By the time I finish my degree I'll be sprouting a whole heap of important words while the planet keeps on dying.

I brush the thought from my mind, breathe in deeply again, return to all that blue. Such a small word, *blue*, for something so incredibly big. And my first word ever, according to Mum, that day on the beach when she and my dad were so rapt to hear me speak. *Blue.* And I'm thinking how if you looked down from a plane you'd be able to see its edges, you could plot it on a map; but from where I'm standing now, it seems to have no end. Maybe tomorrow I can bring Lindsay and we can look at it together. Because, even though we don't always see things in the same way, it's the looking together that matters. Standing close, not saying a word.

And we're only nineteen, the two of us. We have all the time in the world.

But then again, we haven't.

Acknowledgements

My wholehearted thanks to Terri-ann White, the director of UWA Publishing, for continuing to endorse my writing. It's been a great pleasure, the third time around, to work with Terri-ann and her enthusiastic and professional team. A special thanks to Nicola Redhouse for her thoughtful and meticulous editorial eye.

Thanks to my wonderful friends and to my much-loved family: my sons, Jack and Harry, and my husband, Dan, who reads my work intelligently and patiently, and who pushes me to keep drafting and re-drafting and re-drafting. And pushes me again.

And thanks to my mother, for her resilience, courage and good humour. This collection is for you, Mum.

www.ingramcontent.com/pod-product-compliance
Lightning Source LLC
Chambersburg PA
CBHW022110170626
46808CB00002B/675